BACKROAD RAMBLINGS
VOLUME TWO

STORIES OF FAITH, LOVE, AND LAUGHTER

DONNA POOLE

Copyright © 2022 by Donna Poole

All rights reserved worldwide.

No part of this book may be reproduced in any form or by any electronic or mechanical means, including information storage and retrieval systems, without written permission from the author, except for the use of brief quotations in a book review.

Edited by Kimberlee Kiefer

Cover design by SelfPubBookCovers.com/RLSather

ISBN: 9798359100830

"And who will walk a mile with me
Along life's weary way?
A friend whose heart has eyes to see
The stars shine out o'er darkening lea,
And the quiet rest at the end of the day,
A friend who knows and dares to say
The brave, sweet words that cheer the way
Where he walks a mile with me.

With such a comrade, such a friend
I fain would walk till journey's end
Through summer sunshine, winter rain,
And then—farewell, we shall meet again!"
–Henry Van Dyke

I dedicate this book to all my friends in real life and to my book friends who travel with me. Let's treasure friendship, one of God's best gifts, and let's keep walking each other Home.

> "We are all travelers in the wilderness of the world and the best we can find in our travels is an honest friend." –Robert Louis Stevenson

HERE WE GO AGAIN!
JANUARY 2021

Media, especially social media, is gloomier than Michigan in January, and that's saying a lot.

Michigan has many superlatives. For one thing, some claim (but others dispute) we have the longest freshwater coastline in the world. We do have 3,288 miles of it. We're a big old peninsula surrounded by four of the five Great Lakes, and that's wonderful, but all that water causes gloomy, cloudy days in November, December, and January.

If we Michiganders aren't careful, gloom seeps right into our bones and turns us all into Eeyores, the dismal donkey of *Winnie the Pooh* fame.

Media, especially social media, is gloomier than Eeyore, and that's saying a lot.

I saw a meme—we Boomers used to call them cartoons—that made me feel like laughing and crying. A woman jumped out of a window in a burning building labeled 2020, landed on a fireman's trampoline, and catapulted into another window in a burning building tagged 2021.

We get that; don't we? Are we, perhaps, a bit jaded and gloomy after the year we just finished?

And yet, hope remains. It might peek out for only a minute a day, like the Michigan sunshine did on a recent morning; it might be tattered and jagged, but it's there.

I saw bright sunshine amidst Facebook gloom today. A friend posted a Tigger minute: "Addicted to hope."

"Me too!" I commented. It's poor grammar; I know. I should say, "I am also," but "me too!" seemed more cheerful and Tiggerish.

I am addicted to hope.

Hope is why we read mystery books, put together puzzles, or play Spider Solitaire. We like to see complicated, hopeless things come together in a satisfactory conclusion. We long for all the things we aren't finding in current events or perhaps even in our own lives: peace, answers, and everything in its proper place. We're desperate to find that one puzzle piece missing under the table.

Hope sneaks up on us when we smell a trailer load of new lumber, or open a new notebook, or turn the first page of a book. Hope and anticipation are almost inseparable. Many new things inspire hope; there's a reason a new year is often depicted as a baby.

It's hope that makes us try that exercise program in one more effort to rid ourselves of the SpongeBob SquarePants silhouette.

It's hope that makes me pick up my tiny, two-pound weights. I want to regain a little of the strength cancer is stealing. And I want to do something about this skin that kind of lies here next to me in a puddle. I'm sorry about that word picture; blame my niece, Sheri.

Years ago, when she was still in school, Sheri worked at a nursing home.

"I like my patients, but not their skin! It lies there next to them."

Now I'm one of those people; cancer treatments caused me to lose weight too fast. I hope to do something about that skin. What, I don't know, except laugh and remember Sheri.

Laughter aside, I do have serious hopes for 2021, and I'm sure you do too. I know we're all beyond tired of the fighting and the violence. We hope for many things to change in the world and in our lives.

We could easily give into hopelessness when dreams not only shatter around us but almost crush the life out of us when they fall.

Sin and suffering are a creeping darkness enfolding our planet, but even for that, there is hope.

I looked for but can't find the George MacDonald quote where he wrote that sin and her children; sorrow and suffering, are sickly and dying, but joy and her children are strong and will live forever. That's hope!

Faith, hope, and love entwine in a strong three-fold cord in the Christian's heart.[1]

The King James Bible uses the word "hope" 129 times!

Hope is the one thing we can't live without.

My heart paraphrases Psalm 43:5, "Why are you sad and upset, oh my soul? Hope in God!"

Unlike politics, health, exercise programs, or dreams, hope in God is a sure thing. God never fails. For those who know Him, far, far better things are coming than we have the imagination to even begin to hope for.

So, here we go again! So far, 2021 looks as bleak or bleaker than 2020, but only if we leave God and hope out of the equation. That I don't intend to do. I've had enough of cloudy, gloomy days. I'm ready to sit in the sunshine of hope. Anyone want to sit there with me?

IT'S A GIRL! IT'S A BOY! IT'S A BOOK?
JANUARY 2021

"Why couldn't I have sent them to my family instead of to yours?" I worried to my husband, John, after his mom called me.

"Donna, the birth announcements you sent us and our family and friends?"

"Yes?"

I waited, expecting John's mom to praise the patriotic announcements John had chosen, red, white, and blue, with the words, "Our First Lady." Praise wasn't her response.

"You forgot to fill them out. They're empty. No name, no birth weight, nothing."

I apologized profusely. I knew I was tired, but I didn't know I was that tired. Back then I didn't even have the excuse of brain surgery to offer! In my exhaustion, I thought I'd completed all the announcements, but I'd only filled out half of them. My family got the half with the information; John's family got the blank ones.

Two boys and another girl followed "Our First Lady," and I

double-checked to make sure the announcements had the pertinent information before we took them to the post office.

There's nothing like having a new baby, unless it's having a book baby!

Having a baby and writing a book have a few things in common.

Babies and books both arrive with pain. Both keep you awake at night. Both capture your hopes and dreams. Both have minds of their own; there's no pouring them into your mold.

The characters in the books I write are fictional, but they feel real to me. Sometimes, I'll catch just a glimpse of someone who later becomes a major character in my stories. I find inspiration in the people around me and in the stories I read.

I love the broken people in the Bible because I am a broken person. Aren't we all? The ones who are broken, capture my heart with their brokenness because I too have been broken, body, soul, and spirit.

The Pharisee in the Bible story who pounded his chest with pride and thanked God he was not like "this publican," however, was never someone who captured my heart. Instead, I cried and related to the broken publican who heard the Pharisee and wept, "God be merciful to me, a sinner."

The elder brother in the story of the Prodigal Son was also a bit too perfect to be one of my people. I loved the younger son who came trudging up the dusty road, weary in body and spirit, only able to form the words, "Forgive me, Father, for I have sinned."

Sometimes, my characters get lost on their backroad ramblings toward home, and sometimes this author does too. I suppose the same is true of some of my readers. How wonderful to have a loving Father who runs to welcome us when we repent and turn toward Home!

It's a happy time for me when I can announce the birth of a new book baby. In my books, you'll find many broken, imperfect people who are happy to be children of a kind Father. I send them out into the world with prayers they'll help and bless others.

THE FATHER'S BACKYARD
FEBRUARY 2021

Have you been to the Father's Backyard? Some scoff and say it's an imaginary place, but I've been there myself and assure you it's more real than anywhere else I've ever been.

It's a more beautiful backyard than you can imagine in your best dreams; the sun always smiles, and the grass makes a year-round carpet for bare feet. People say there's a house just over the hill called "The Father's House." But none of us have ever seen the house or the Father, only the Father's mailbox, and His backyard, perfect for adults who haven't forgotten how to play.

Artists gather daily in the Father's Backyard to play at their work. Phyllis perfects her photography. Patrick paints with oils and watercolors. Weston weaves lovely patterns from lamb's wool. Grace grows lovely flowers and vegetables in her garden. Archie designs architectural marvels. Bella practices ballet as Orville leads an orchestra. Sarah sculpts statues that decorate the garden while Wilson writes beautiful stories. Caleb makes masterpieces with his carpentry skills. Catherine creates meals that feed body and soul.

Newest to the group and greatly loved is young Paul whose poetry captures dreams and turns them into words. He often reads his poems aloud, and creativity being contagious, the work of the others becomes even more beautiful.

In groups and in solitude, artists use the gifts the Father has given them to enrich the lives of the rest. Every evening, as the magic hour of twilight falls, each artist stops creating and admires the work of the others. There is no envy. The one who sings like an angel doesn't wish to be the ornithologist cataloging the beautiful birds. The writer in the wheelchair never envies the ballerina.

The artists end each day relaxing around a campfire, contented with their work and proud of each other. They talk softly, draw warmth from the crackling flames and from friendship, and watch the first stars appear. Then they stop by the Father's mailbox, go home to sleep, and return refreshed the next day to play at their work again in the Father's Backyard.

I remember the day things changed.

Paul's poems had always been a bit melancholy, but no one minded. Sorrow and tears added beauty to all our work and reminded us we were only in the Father's Backyard, not yet at His house. But Paul's poems began to take on an eerie darkness.

It seemed he'd forgotten what Helen Keller had often said when she'd played in the Father's Backyard in her day,

> "Although the world is full of suffering, it is full also of the overcoming of it."

Paul's poems had sometimes reminded me of the beautiful face of a baby who smiles through tears on his cheeks or of a rainbow after a storm when the sun breaks through the clouds. Now there was no smile, no sun, only tears and storm clouds.

There was no overcoming left in Paul's poetry. When he read it aloud, the other artists' hands and minds grew heavy.

Then Paul stopped writing. Day after day he sat with his chin in his hands and refused to talk or to be comforted. Not even the warmth of the evening campfire helped.

I wasn't the only one who caught my breath in horror when Paul came to say goodbye. His face looked like an ancient oak; he shuffled slowly, and he bent from the waist and could no longer stand upright. His entire back looked like it was covered with lumps.

"I can't come to the Father's Backyard anymore," Paul said. "It's too painful. I have nothing left to give, and your beautiful work makes me bitter."

And then Paul pitched face forward. He was still breathing, but barely.

Doctor Dan rushed to help. "I've seen this only once before here in the Father's Backyard, but I think I recognize this poison."

"Poison?" I stared at him. "Someone is poisoning Paul?"

"Not someone, something," Doctor Dan said as he removed Paul's shirt.

Paul's back was covered with layers of sticky notes. Doctor Dan began pulling them off.

"Quickly, please help me," he said to those of us who were standing close to Paul.

"What are these?" I asked as I yanked off notes.

"Something too heavy for any artist to carry. Something the rest of us leave in the Father's mailbox every night before we go home."

I glanced at the notes in my hands.

I recognized the words on one of them; they were my own: "Paul, your poetry captures dreams and turns them into words."

I read a few more, all of them praise, most in prose far more eloquent than my own.

"A man is tested by his praise," Doctor Dan muttered grimly as he kept working. "Who was responsible for this man's orientation?"

We looked at each other. No one had told Paul about the mailbox? The poor man had been hoarding praise, keeping all those compliments for himself?

Doctor Dan pulled the last of the notes from Paul's back. Paul stirred and began to cry. The sun shone through his tears and made a rainbow.

We drifted off to our work-play as Doctor Dan quietly told Paul about the Father's mailbox and how each night before we went home we whispered Psalm 115:1 and put into the mailbox all the praise given to us that day.

Paul was weak, content to sit in the sun, feel the grass carpet under his bare feet, and eat the nourishing soup Catherine created for him. That night we began a new tradition around the campfire.

As the flames died down to embers, we stood, hands clasped over our hearts, and chanted Psalm 115:1 together:

"Not unto us, O Lord, not unto us, but unto thy name
     give glory, for thy mercy, and for thy truth's sake."

I was young then, and now I am old. I haven't seen another case of praise poison almost destroy an artist, but just in case someone else misses the orientation, we still recite our fireside chant. Paul, our beautiful old poet laureate, reminds us to stop by the Father's mailbox and place all praise there before we leave each night.

And that is how our souls stay young and light enough to laugh and create. Our bodies slow and sag, but we are still joyful children, playing in the Father's Backyard.

Come join us!

BY THE SKIN OF MY TEETH
FEBRUARY 2021

The patient sits next to me working on his physical therapy exercises.

"I just might get this blog written and posted this week by the skin of my teeth," I say to John.

He answers with a groan. Even the heavy-duty medications can't erase the pain of his exercises today.

"Now it's time to get back on your CPM."

My kind, loving, normally cheerful Valentine glares at me.

"I just got off it."

"You still have four hours to go."

People warned us that total knee replacement surgery wasn't easy. John's surgery was Monday; he came home Thursday, and he had his first home physical therapy session yesterday. He's hurting today. But he's glad to be home, and I'm happy he's here. He's home for Valentine's Day, home by the skin of his teeth.

John had a painful, weak day near the end of his hospital stay. When it took three nurses to get him adjusted on his controlled passive motion (CPM) machine, we both wondered if he should consider inpatient rehab. It wasn't our first choice, but we weren't sure he could handle coming home. We prayed about it, and John told me to call our local rehab center to see if they had room for him.

"I'm sorry; we don't. We're only taking Covid patients this week."

We were relieved, and John felt like he'd escaped going to rehab by the skin of his teeth.

Isn't language fascinating? I love exploring the history of old sayings. "By the skin of my teeth" means "I managed it but only by a narrow margin." People use the ancient phrase to express an escape or an achievement that barely happened. It's a distance too small to measure.

The Geneva Bible of 1559 was the first to use the expression in Job 19:20:

"I haue escaped with the skinne of my tethe."

I avoided being fired once by the skin of my teeth. I sold flight insurance at the Broome County Airport in Binghamton, New York. Joy, my boss, flew in occasionally from New York City. I always heard her coming by the brisk click, click, click of her high heels on the terminal's tile. She was tall and lovely with perfect make up, and she made me want to throw up. Not because she was so perfect, but because I knew she was going to yell at me.

During training, Joy taught me the tricks of selling flight insurance: how to subtly play on the fear of first-time flyers, how to appeal to a senior citizen's love of a grandchild, how to "sell up." Our policies ranged from twenty-five cents to five-hundred dollars, but Joy warned us never to sell a twenty-five-cent policy.

"What if someone asks what our cheapest policy is?" another trainee asked.

Joy said, "Start out selling high. Come down to twenty-five dollars, only if you must. If a customer asks for the cheapest say, 'Well, we also have ones for ten and five dollars.' I will fire anyone who sells a twenty-five-cent insurance policy!"

Day after day, I sold twenty-five-cent policies. Many of them. When someone asked for our cheapest, I sold our cheapest.

"Joy is going to be furious," the long-time employees warned me.

And Joy was furious. Every time she came, she hollered at me and warned me it better never happen again, but she didn't fire me. She often threatened to. She demanded my reasons. I explained my ethics. She looked puzzled and shook her head.

"I think you have potential to be one of my top salespeople. Try to sell a lifetime five-hundred-dollar policy before I come back. It doesn't matter if the person will never fly again. I'll feel good about you selling it."

I shook my head. I wouldn't do it, and she knew it. She sighed.

"I'm going to have to fire you one of these days, Donna Piarulli. You know that, don't you?"

I loved every job I ever had except that one. I was so relieved to give my notice when John and I were going to get married and move out of state.

On my last day of work, Joy threw me a wedding shower. The decorations were beautiful, the food delicious, and the cake amazing. I felt overwhelmed by the generous gifts, especially the lavish ones from Joy.

Joy had to leave the shower early to catch her flight back home to New York City. I walked her to her gate and thanked her. She bent down and hugged me.

"You do know, Donna Piarulli, that I would have had to fire you eventually, don't you?"

"I know."

Then we looked at each other and laughed. Joy flew off to New York City, and I never saw her again. I ended up living on a dirt road in Michigan, happy not to be a big city boss who only escaped by the skin of her teeth from having to fire someone she really liked.

Speaking of by the skin of my teeth, we once knew a man who made it to heaven only by the skin of his teeth. He was dying in the hospital, and his family asked John to go see him. John asked him if he'd ever repented of his sin and accepted God's gift of salvation.

"Jesus died on the cross to take the punishment we deserve for sin," John explained. "We only need to believe He died in our place and accept His gift of eternal life."

The man replied, "I did that when I was a kid."

John looked troubled when he told me about it.

"He was lying, honey; I know it."

The man's son-in-law burst into the auditorium on Sunday when John was preaching.

"Can you come quick, Pastor? Dad's dying and asking for you."

A deacon finished the service, and John hurried to the hospital. The man could barely talk.

He managed only two words, his last: "I lied."

"You lied when you told me you had asked Jesus to save you from sin and give you eternal life?"

The man nodded, looking terrified and miserable.

"Squeeze my hand if you're praying this with me. Dear Father, I know I'm a sinner and I'm sorry. I don't deserve heaven."

The man clutched John's hand.

"I believe Jesus took my punishment for sin when He died on the cross. I accept what He did in my place. I thank You for the gift of eternal life."

The man squeezed John's hand again. John looked at his peaceful, smiling face.

"Do you know where you're going when you die?"

The man nodded and squeezed John's hand one last time. He died quietly a few hours later and opened his eyes in heaven. He made it by the skin of his teeth.

SNOW STORY
FEBRUARY 2021

I have a fireplace, cozy throws, warm drinks, and some snow stories to tell, if you're interested. We were snowbound this morning. This is the first storm when I haven't bundled up and walked out through deep drifts. I'm not strong enough yet for that, but I did go from window to window, as excited as a child. I love freshly fallen snow undisturbed by footprints, shovels, or plows.

Even John, home from the hospital after knee replacement surgery, used his walker to hobble to the window and exclaim over how much snow fell overnight. If our neighbor hadn't plowed us out, we'd still be snowed in.

Spring energizes the poets, but so does snow. Think of some of the songs, idioms, and hymns inspired by snow:

- "Let it Snow" –the coziness of being snowed in with someone you love
- "Where are the snows of yesteryear?" –a nostalgic sadness for time past
- "Snow on the roof" –white hair

- "Snowball into something" –growing quickly larger like a snowball being rolled
- "Snowed under" –overwhelmed with work
- "Pure as the driven snow" –a person of high integrity
- "Get snowed" –to be deceived
- "Snowbird" –someone who heads south in winter months
- "Whiter than Snow"—a hymn describing forgiveness

Here are a few idioms I didn't understand until I looked them up. To "roast snow in a furnace" means to attempt something impossible. "Snow stuff" and "Lady Snow" mean cocaine.

John is allergic to codeine and before knee surgery he laughingly told the nurse anesthesiologist about the time he'd confused his words and had told a doctor he was allergic to cocaine.

"Some people are, you know," the nurse replied, "and we need to know that, because we sometimes use it as an anesthetic."

I thought the nurse might be giving us a snow job, but he was serious, and a Mayo Clinic web search confirmed what he'd said.

We were so glad to get John home from the hospital before the snowstorm hit. When the storm started, I wanted to post Dean Martin's version of "Let It Snow" on my Facebook page, but I didn't have time. I was too snowed under from taking care of John. If you're still reading this, you're either chuckling or groaning at the way these idioms are snowballing.

This storm's snow piled up quickly and reminded me of the blizzard of 1978, but we didn't have the winds we did then, and when you live in open farm country, it's the winds that close roads. In 1978, the winds wouldn't quit; they howled over the open fields, scooped up the snow, and dumped it on the roads. We were snowbound for three weeks. At first it was fun and cozy; we'd been way too busy, and it was wonderful reconnecting as a family. But eventually we got cabin fever; we missed the outside world, church, and friends. We missed people!

We felt almost delighted when a snowmobile sunk in a huge drift in front of our house. On it was a person, a real live person! John helped him dig out his machine and invited him in for hot chocolate. We asked him what was open in the rest of the county. His reply was brief.

"Nothin'."

Another day, a loud knock on the door startled us. We opened it to see a smiling, snow covered, half-frozen friend from church, George Fee. He pulled off his gloves, shoved a hand in his pocket, and pulled out a wad of cash.

"Here you go, Pastor. I figured you might be needing some money. We haven't had church in weeks, so I know you haven't been paid."

"But George," John asked, "where did you get the money? And how did you get here?"

"Well, I drove to the homes of church folks who live on main roads and asked them, 'You got any money for the preacher?' And I got all this!" George grinned, proud of himself. "And how I got here was I left my car parked out on Squawfield Road and hiked in through the fields. There's more snow on the roads than in the fields!"

A few days after George came, we got more company. Like George, they left their car on Squawfield and walked to our house through the fields. Our good friends, Pastor Potter and Audrey, and their son came to visit. Pastor unzipped his coat, and we all laughed. Their tiny poodle, Buttons, poked out his little nose.

The four of them, three humans and a dog, stayed for supper and spent the night. We stayed up late, laughing, talking, and playing games. Someone had the idea of rewriting the Luke 15:11-32 story of the Prodigal Son. We wrote it in "The Key of D."

I can't remember all of it, but we thought we were hysterical as we wrote, "The despicable dude departed his dad's domain...."

The later it got, the funnier we thought we were.

Where are the snows of yesteryear? Yes, I feel a nostalgic sadness as I tell you the story of the night we spent with our friends. We were young then and getting old seemed so far away.

Now, those of us still alive have snow on the roof. Buttons crossed the rainbow bridge long ago, and Pastor Potter is in heaven.

That man could preach, and that man could sing! I'm sure he sang "Whiter Than Snow" many times, and preached Isaiah 1:18:

> "Come now, and let us reason together, saith the
> > LORD: though your sins be as scarlet, they shall be as white as snow; though they be red like crimson, they shall be as wool."

I miss the snows of yesteryear; so many people I love are already in heaven. The best really is yet to be, and I'm looking forward to it!

But before we go to heaven, anyone want to write the Prodigal Son in "The Key of C?" I have a fireplace, cozy throws, and warm drinks if you want to get the party started.

THE SPARROW AND THE GRUMPY ANGEL
FEBRUARY 2021

"**G**oodbye, honey," I whispered, seeing the tears in John's eyes and blinking back my own.

We both knew I was in God's care and the expertise of a top brain surgeon, but it was still difficult to let go of hands and be separated, one to face surgery the other to spend hours waiting for news.

When I let go of John's hand, I slipped my hand into God's hand, and the beautiful flute music my friend Vicky had played at church the day before drifted through my thoughts:

"His eye is on the sparrow, and I know He cares
  for me."

God did care for me. Eight years ago, yesterday, God brought me through a craniotomy for a brain aneurysm. It left thirteen pieces of hardware in my head and some synthetic dura covering my brain. I had hydrocephalus, but the fluid buildup was mild. My surgeon left the choice up to me: have an additional surgery to put in a shunt, or go home and let my body heal itself.

"Your body will absorb the fluid, but you'll have horrible headaches," Dr. Thompson warned me.

"I just want to go home."

He chuckled. "I knew that's what you were going to say."

Home I went. I'm allergic to pain medications, so I couldn't take any. The headaches were horrendous, and my dreams were vivid. Every night, in my dreams, an angel rowed up to the shore where I waited. We didn't say anything to each other. I got into the boat, and he rowed me out onto a calm, black lake. It was wonderfully quiet on the lake in the darkness of midnight; no stars or moon ever appeared in my nightly dreams. I rested on something soft in the bottom of the boat, my head on a pillow. The pain that tortured me when I was awake dared not follow me into that sacred place.

Once, I trailed my hand through the water. It was warm and soothing.

"No!" the angel scolded. "Put your hand back in the boat. It's not safe yet."

Before daylight, the angel rowed me back to shore.

Gradually, I began feeling better, but I kept dreaming the same thing every night for six weeks. The last night I dreamt it, I waited on the shore, and the silent angel rowed up as usual. I hesitated, looking at the boat, then back at the land.

"Well, are you getting in or not?"

I was shocked.

God's angels are grumpy?

Apparently, some are.

"No, I don't think I'm coming tonight."

"Fine. But I'm not coming back for seven years."

I puzzled over that dream for a while. I'm not one who

thinks every dream means something, but the same dream every night for six weeks had to say something to me.

Had the angel in my dream been the death angel? I didn't think so; why would he take me home every night before sunrise if he were? I finally decided the dream was reminding me that regardless of pain, the One whose eye is on the sparrow would give me rest. But what did the seven years mean? I didn't have a clue.

Seven years came. Nothing happened. Seven years and three months passed, and I found out I had cancer. When the chemotherapy began and my old friend pain returned, so did the dream. The angel doesn't come every night in my dreams, but he comes sometimes. I'm happy to see him; I get into the boat, lie down, and rest. I know God's eye is on the sparrow, and I know He cares for me.

However dark the night, however searing the pain, God sees His children. He knows, and He cares. He can stop the pain, and sometimes He does. Why doesn't He always?

Oh, we all know the pat answers, and they are true. Pain is a great teacher.

But we will never fully understand the why of some of the horrendous things that happen to God's people. When a family is ripped apart by devastation more sudden than a tornado from a midwestern sky, caught in a whirlwind of agony, what then? God's children grasp for anything then to keep from being pulled into a pit of despair so deep there is no return. The blessed ones find the wild winds slamming them up against the cross.

We can't fully understand all that took place on the cross either, but we can comprehend what we need to know.

There, Jesus said, "It is finished."

On the cross, Jesus conquered pain, sin, death, and hell. The empty tomb assures us the day is coming when He will wipe away all tears from His children's eyes, and sorrow will be swallowed up in joy.

But that day isn't here yet, is it?

Until then, I need the reminder of the sparrow and my grumpy angel.

The angel isn't any more talkative now than he was all those years ago. Is he still grumpy? I don't know because we haven't exchanged a word. Maybe I'll dream I put my hand in the water again and see how he reacts. If he yells at me, I'll let you know.

LION AND LAMB
MARCH 2021

I wish I knew what Mom was like as a kid. She didn't talk much about her childhood, other than to say her dad beat her with a razor strap, and I was too busy being a kid myself to ask her questions. I could have asked her only sibling, Uncle Tom. He was twelve years older than she was; I'm sure he could have told us stories about her. Mom was born in March; did she arrive like a lion? I imagine her being a lion. Mom died in March, and I know she died like a lamb.

The mom of my childhood years was more lion than lamb; we didn't often see the gentle, more affectionate side of her. I used to mutter she'd make a good drill sergeant, or prosecuting attorney, or a general. Mom never cried and was proud of that and impatient with the tears of others. She was exacting in her demands that we keep the house spotless.

Mom did love us, but her love often expressed itself in anger: anger when she couldn't find us when we got lost on our bikes, anger when we ducked when she reached to fix a stray lock of our hair, and anger when we dared to disobey.

Mom could wield a belt with more skill than Zorro with a sword.

They say the Pharisees of Jesus' day had 613 rules in addition to the biblical ones; Mom had at least 6,130!

And I didn't like any of them.

We knew where we stood with Mom. She drew her lines sharp and clear, and I usually stood on the wrong side of them. Poor Mom. She didn't know what to do with me.

When shouting and spankings failed to achieve her desired results, she often said the one thing that sent cold chills down my little girl spine: "I wish the worst possible thing I can think of for you. I hope when you grow up you have a little girl who acts just like you do."

Even as a child, I knew that was a curse I didn't want fulfilled.

Please God, no, not a little girl like me.

We had four wonderful children, and though they weren't the angel my husband was growing up—according to his mom—neither were they the little devil I was! See why I believe in grace and mercy?

When Mom was in her late forties, and I was twenty, she had a major stroke that paralyzed her right side and left her unable to speak. She regained her speech and limited use of her right leg but none of her right arm or hand.

The most striking change was Mom's personality. Our lion became a lamb: gentle, emotional, and loving. Life was difficult for Mom for the next five years until God allowed a second major stroke to carry her home to heaven.

I'm glad I got to know both of my moms, the lion, and the lamb. We all have a bit of each, don't we?

When March comes in like a lion and goes out like a lamb, I think of Mom. When March comes in like a lamb and goes out like a lion, I think of Mom.

Jesus is called both the Lamb of God and the Lion of the tribe of Judah. He came to earth the first time as a Lamb, meek and willing to give His life as a sacrifice for our sins. When His feet touch the earth the second time He'll come as a Lion, ready to conquer all evil and set up His glorious kingdom of joy and peace.

When March comes in like a lion and goes out like a lamb, I think of Jesus. When March comes in like a lamb and goes out like a lion, I think of Jesus.

Evil, hatred, and cruelty may triumph now, but their tyrannical reign is crumbling. The day is coming when right here on earth the lion will lie down with the lamb, and a little child will be safe with all God's creatures.[1]

When Mom and I meet again, I wonder if we'll remember her curse and laugh. Her angry lion days have already ended, and my days of defiantly standing on the wrong side of the line will end when I get where Mom is now. My breaking of her 6,130 rules will be forgotten, and there will be nothing left between us but love.

EYE OF THE HURRICANE
MARCH 2021

She's capricious; kind one day, malevolent the next. We're foolish to trust her, but year after year she captures us with her charms. Who can resist the reddening of bushes on the backroads, tiny leaves on lilacs, the cry of the red-wings, or evening magic of spring peepers? She gives us all these, but she sometimes slams us with ice storms or blizzards.

She's Michigan March. She's like the eye of a hurricane, tricking us into thinking the danger of winter storms is gone.

I have a writer friend with recurrent ovarian cancer. She calls her between treatment times the eye of the hurricane.

I'm in the eye of the hurricane right now as I wait for the results of my fourth PET scan.

"Can't you get it right this time?" I asked the PET scan tech. "You guys keep messing up, and I have to keep coming back for another one."

He chuckled, once I explained I was joking.

As they fastened my head firmly between wedges and

strapped me to the narrow scan table, I asked the two techs, "Can you help me find a friend I lost in here?"

I couldn't move my head to see them, but I could feel the looks they were giving each other.

Oh boy, here we go; she's the crazy one of the day.

"Um, you lost a friend, ma'am? In here? In this room?"

"I sure did! His name is NED! Have either of you seen him?"

Long silence.

I imagined their thoughts: *Do we call psych before or after the scan? How well do we have her strapped down?*

"You guys know NED! Lots of people have discovered him in this room, but I haven't found him yet. He's an acronym for No Evidence of Disease!"

One tech laughed, relieved. "Oh! NED! I think he's going to be my new best friend!"

"Mine too!" I said, as they slid me back into the machine.

Arms in an uncomfortable position over my head, I still managed to fall asleep.

That's my shining claim to fame, being able to sleep anywhere. Once I fell asleep while talking on the phone to my daughter, Angie, and terrified her. When I didn't answer her, she thought I'd had another stroke.

I've fallen asleep in church. I know lots of people have done that, but how many of them are the pastor's wife?

Not only did I fall asleep during the scan, I made a funny noise, woke up, and jumped. You aren't supposed to move in those scans, but they said I hadn't messed up the images.

As I got ready to leave, I asked the poor tech if he'd found NED. It was unkind of me to ask; I knew they weren't allowed to give any information to patients.

"I didn't really see all your pictures...."

"It's okay." I smiled at him. "If you didn't find NED this time, you can help me look for him next time."

"That's the spirit! If we didn't find him today, we'll help you find him next time."

And now.

Now I wait for results. Did the cancer shrink or spread? Did they—glorious thought—did they find NED?

If NED is still winning at this hide and seek game, what comes next? So many questions, and only God knows the answers. He gives us hints in March.

I held my daughter's arm the other day. Kimmee and I walked around the yard looking for March signs of early spring. The lovely snowdrop flowers bloom first. We found rhubarb and tulips bravely forcing their way out of darkness into light. We saw trees full of birds singing loudly in a decibel competition. We felt the warm sunlight on our faces.

A bone-chilling blizzard might still come. An ice storm may make the birds wish they'd stayed south a bit longer, but spring, real spring will come. It always does.

The storms always return too, sometimes with a fierceness that freezes tears. What then? Which is true? Spring's softness or her dangers? Both are true. How do we reconcile it; how do we understand?

What about life's suffering: crushed hopes, unbearable pain, and the death of kittens, children, young brides, and old grandparents. How do we understand that? We don't.

We cling to God's love and the fact an eternal spring will win in the end.

The only thing that can thaw our frozen hearts when suffering and tragedy destroy hope is the cross. We don't judge God's love by how we feel or by circumstances we face; we can't understand any of that. We evaluate God's love by one thing only: Calvary.

I don't know if softness or danger is coming to me, but meanwhile I'm resting in the eye of the hurricane and loving every bit of spring I find.

> "God, make me brave for life: oh, braver than this.
> Let me straighten after pain, as a tree straightens after the rain,
> Shining and lovely again.
> God, make me brave for life; much braver than this.
> As the blown grass lifts, let me rise from sorrow with quiet eyes,
> Knowing Thy way is wise.
> God, make me brave, life brings such blinding things.
> Help me to keep my sight; help me to see aright
> That out of the dark comes light." –Unknown

LET'S GO FOR A WALK
MARCH 2021

Late afternoon shadows lengthened; mama robins sang soft lullabies to babies cradled in nests, and all the world began gentling for the night. Twilight was E's favorite time of the day. It was almost time for his evening walk.

Every evening, E's walking partner arrived. The two of them rambled along the backroads, talking over the day's events, admiring the paintings in the sky, or sometimes walking in comfortable silence. E felt most himself on these walks, most understood, most at home. When they arrived back at E's home and his walking partner left him and walked alone off into the distance, E felt a pang of regret as he watched him go.

One day, the two friends walked farther than they ever had before. E realized they were on an unfamiliar and strangely beautiful country road. The breeze caressing his face smelled sweet, like something from a half-forgotten dream. He'd never seen such a vibrant sunset, and when it faded, the stars appeared so close E impulsively reached his hand up to touch them.

His walking partner laughed.

"We've walked a long way this time, and it's getting late. We're closer to my home than we are to yours now. Do you want to come home with me?"

E had never wanted anything more.

The Bible puts it this way:

> "And Enoch walked with God: and he was not; for God took him." –Genesis 5:24

I think that's one of the loveliest stories in the Bible. I'd love to go for a walk with God on our country road and just keep walking on to heaven, but not quite yet.

I don't know how close to heaven I am. We'd hoped to find my friend, NED (No Evidence of Disease), in my recent PET scan, but he eluded us again. Morticia, my lymphoma lung tumor, is still active; although, my radiation oncologist thinks she's shrinking. He still gives me a twenty percent chance of living. On Thursday, I'll visit my chemotherapy oncologist and see if he thinks more chemo can possibly kill off stubborn Morticia, who has lived in my lung almost a year now without paying a cent of rent and has in general made a nuisance of herself.

Lest I be unfair to Morticia, she has given me some gifts too. One of them is an appreciation of every day I get to walk on this earth with God, my family, and my friends.

Despite how man has mishandled it, this earth is still incredibly lovely. We haven't yet disfigured it beyond the point of being able to see in it the face of our Creator.

And isn't life a breathtakingly wonderful yet fragile gift? Morticia tells me that every day. Each time I've done anything this last year I've been poignantly aware it may be the last time. That's not a morbid way to live; it's beautiful. It makes everything so deeply meaningful. I only wish I'd been aware of this gift years before Morticia handed it to me.

I want to leave precious memories for my loved ones, not so they remember me dying, but so they remember me living life fully and loving them unconditionally.

So, thank you, Morticia, for all that. And now that I have your gifts, you can leave. For good. I won't miss you; I promise.

Tim McGraw sings, "Live Like You Were Dying," and it would be wonderful if we could only do that without a Morticia to remind us.

I want to stay here to see all my grandchildren grow up and my children grow old. I'd like to someday retire to a quiet little place with John. But when my time comes to die, I'd like to go when late afternoon shadows lengthen; mama robins sing soft lullabies to babies cradled in nests, and all the world begins gentling for the night. I'll be waiting then for God to come walk me Home.

PIG PLEASE NO BLOAT
MARCH 2021

I was only a thought of God, four years from being born, when Bing Crosby crooned "Swinging on a Star" in 1944. I loved singing that song when I was a kid; I especially liked the verse about the pig. I giggled when I sang:

> Or would you like to swing on a star
> Carry moonbeams home in a jar
> And be better off than you are
> Or would you rather be a pig?
> A pig is an animal with dirt on his face
> His shoes are a terrible disgrace
> He has no manners when he eats his food
> He's fat and lazy and extremely rude
> But if you don't care a feather or a fig
> You may grow up to be a pig.

I little guessed then that when I became an old lady, I'd want to be a pig... a guinea pig that is.

A guinea pig isn't really a pig; it's a rodent. Though not

often used now for scientific experiments, guinea pigs were common subjects from the seventeenth through part of the twentieth centuries. They played an important role in medical research; in 1890, scientists used them to find the antitoxin for diphtheria, and who knows how many millions of lives that spared?

Since 1920, "guinea pig" has been a metaphor for anyone involved in a scientific experiment, and now I hope to be one.

Don't be alarmed, I'm sane, well as sane as I ever was. I'm not off my rocker yet. That's another fascinating idiom, don't you think? It's been around since the late 1800s and may have originated with the idea of an older person being so unstable that he or she fell out of the rocking chair.

So, why do I aspire to be a rodent? Doctor K, my chemotherapy oncologist at University of Michigan hospital, hopes to get me accepted into a drug trial called BiTE. It's only in its second phase, so the study is far from complete, but it looks promising for people with certain cancers, including lymphoma, that stubbornly resist other treatments.

Doctor K showed me my latest PET scan. He doesn't think radiation helped; he thinks Morticia, my stubborn lung tumor looks bigger than ever. Since I'm considered chemo and radiation resistant, treatment options are limited. He told me about the drug trial.

"If I were you, I'd go for it," he said.

I hope they accept me. I haven't heard yet. So once again, we wait; we pray, and we live each day God gives us. This is the God who loves each one of us as though He had only one to love, the God who calls each star by name.

I don't know if this new drug will help me or not; if it doesn't, maybe my participation will help someone who comes after me who also has a stubborn Morticia.

I've done a bit of research about BiTE, and my daughter,

Kimmee, and I were discussing some of the not so pleasant side effects.

"I hope I don't get the bloat," I said.

Kimmee laughed so hard she could barely talk. "Mom! All these horrible side effects and all you can say is you hope you don't get 'the bloat?'"

Yep. That's it. I'd like to swing on a few more stars, be better off than I "are," see some more beautiful springs, and sit around many more crackling campfires with family and friends. To do that, I'll be a pig, guinea that is.

But I don't want the bloat—said tongue-in-cheek. That idiom you can look up yourself.

Thank you for walking all these backroads with me, and happy spring!

THE LITTLE WHITE COAT—ELI PART ONE
MARCH 2021

Eli tugged on the old one's hand. "Listen, Bubbe! Do you hear all the shouting? Can we go see what is happening?"

"I will never finish at the market at this rate," the old one grumbled. But the grandmother's eyes looked as curious as Eli's did. "I wonder what the commotion is. Pontius Pilate has already arrived in Jerusalem with his army of soldiers showing his strength, lest we revolt during Passover."

The old one pushed her tongue into her cheek as a sign of contempt and spat on the dirt, then looked fearfully around hoping none of the Roman governor's men had seen her.

Eli was not afraid. "I wish we would revolt!" he shouted as only a seven-year-old can, stomping his foot. "This is God's land. God's people should rule it, not the Romans. I hate the Romans!"

"Hush, child! Do you learn that Zealot talk at synagogue school? I will forbid you to go if I hear any more!"

The old one cuffed his ears before he could get his hands up to protect them. She was furious because she was afraid for him, he knew. But hadn't the holy Scriptures promised a Messiah, someone who would free them from foreign oppression? He wished he were big enough. He would fight those Romans.

The noise of the crowd was getting louder.

"Please, Bubbe, can we go see?" he begged.

"We will go. But do not get that coat dirty."

With her rough hand she smoothed the white coat she had made for the boy. She knew she hit the child too often, but she'd burned candles many nights spinning wool for the coat for this boy she loved more than life itself.

Soon, the two found themselves in a huge crowd that propelled them forward. It stopped occasionally as people cut branches from palm trees.

They waved the branches in the air and shouted, "Hosanna! Save us now! Blessed is he who comes in the name of the Lord, the king of Israel!"

Eli caught his breath. "Bubbe! Do you hear? It is the Messiah, come to set us free! Now those Roman scoundrels will run for the hills! I want to see our king!"

Eli jumped up and down, trying to see over the heads of the adults packed in around him.

The old one is tall. What is she seeing?

"He is no king," Bubbe scoffed. "He is riding on a donkey's colt and has not even one weapon."

"Then it surely is him, Bubbe! In school we learned the prophet Zechariah said our king would come riding on a donkey's colt!"

The old one frowned at him, still skeptical, but hope lit her eyes.

What kind of child is this to remember words from a dry prophet who had lived hundreds of years ago?

Now people were throwing palm branches onto the road to

make a carpet for the king to ride on. Some were tossing their coats and cloaks on top of the branches to honor their king, their Messiah.

For a brief moment, the crowd parted, and the man on the donkey looked deep into Eli's soul and smiled. For the first time, the little boy knew what it was to worship, to have so much joy and wonder spill up out of your heart your hands must give what they have. Quickly, he shrugged out of his white coat and darted through the crowd. Just as he was ready to throw it down for this wonderful man, this king, he felt his arm wrenched up behind his back.

"What are you doing, you ungrateful wretch of a boy?" The old one snatched his coat from him and boxed an ear. "You will take the coat I went without sleep to make you and throw it in the dirt for this stranger?"

Tears filled Eli's eyes as he looked up at the king.

The donkey stopped. The man bent down.

"Eli El-Bethel always remember this. What you would do, if you could do, in the eyes of God you have already done. Your heavenly Father thanks you."

Then the man looked at the old one. "Martha El-Bethel, God will use this lad in His kingdom. You have loved him well, but fewer ear boxings and more hugs would please the Father."

The donkey moved on. Stunned, Eli and the old one stared at each other.

"Your name is Martha? I did not know that. How did that man know our names? Is he a king? Do you think he is the Messiah? I am sure he is!"

The old one said nothing. She stared after the man with a look on her face Eli had never seen before. She raised her hand, and Eli ducked, but she merely stroked his cheek. Then she put an arm around his shoulders, and the two of them walked home in silence.

Eli didn't say anything because he couldn't erase the face of the man from his vision or stop hearing his words: "What you would do, if you could do, in the eyes of God you have already done. Your heavenly Father thanks you."

Bubbe did not say a word because she was doing something Eli had never seen her do before. She was crying.

> "Among the weeds, the torn debris
> Of strife, of weeping life,
> In hearts struck low,
> A tiny flower grows.
> Its name is Hope."
> –Donna Poole

ELI'S NIGHTMARE FRIDAY—ELI
PART TWO
APRIL 2021

"Bubbe, what do you think the king is doing?" the child asked a hundred times a day.

The old one tried to be patient. She remembered the words of the man they'd met on Sunday, the one Eli insisted was king, the Messiah come to free Israel from Roman rule.

The man had leaned down from his donkey and had spoken to her about Eli: "Martha El-Bethel, God will use this lad in His kingdom. You have loved him well, but fewer ear boxings and more hugs would please the Father."

She had boxed Eli's ears only once since that Sunday. But that one time, not only had she boxed Eli's ears, she had also cuffed the ears of the ancient one, her own father. She shuddered and covered her face with her wrinkled hands, remembering.

Eli had begged to put the ancient one at the table with them instead of at the little table where she usually sat him. His hands shook so much; he spilled every other bite and watching him eat destroyed her appetite. For years, he'd eaten at his own table in silence.

What had come over Eli that he had insisted the ancient one sit next to him at their table?

She still didn't know.

She had given in and had helped her father to a chair. She had avoided looking at him eat, but she had been able to hear his noisy chewing with the few teeth he had left, and it had driven her mad. Still, she had said nothing. But when the ancient one's trembling hands had knocked the cruet of goat's milk into the loaf of bread she had worked so hard making, something had snapped. She had screamed at both him and Eli, had slapped Eli's face and ears, and then had turned her rage on her father, doing the same to him.

Even as she had beaten the ancient one's face, she had remembered words from the Law about honoring one's parents, but they had not stopped her. Eli's crying, pulling her robe, and begging her to beat him instead of the ancient one had not stopped her.

What finally had stopped her were the tears of despair running down the wrinkles in her father's swarthy cheeks and his pleas to Jehovah: "Let me die, merciful One. Let me die."

She had paused, fist raised, and had cried out to Jehovah herself: "Let me die too, or make me a new woman. I despise this person I have become."

She had bathed her father's and Eli's faces with a cloth dipped into warm water as her tears had dripped down over her hands.

Now they both ducked when she raised a hand to fix their hair, a gesture that cut her to the heart, but one she knew she deserved.

Eli stopped sleeping on his mat. Each night, when he thought Bubbe was sleeping, he crept to the ancient one's mat and curled up close to him. Martha heard him talking about the king.

"He is going to free us from the Romans, I know he is! And I think he is going to do more than that. I think he is going to change people. Maybe he will make even Bubbe kind, and then your life will be better. Do not cry! Are you cold? Let me cover you with my robe. I do not need it. Little boys do not get as cold as ancient ones."

Martha half expected Eli to refuse when she asked if he wanted to go to market with her on Friday.

"Will the ancient one be alright alone, Bubbe? He has been sleeping a lot lately."

"He will be fine. He has happy dreams of better days when he sleeps. Perhaps he dreams of your king."

"I will come to the market then! Maybe we will see the king again! I only saw him once, Bubbe, but I love him with all my heart."

Eli slipped his hand into Bubbe's as they walked, and for the second time that week, she felt something she had not felt in more years than she could count. She'd felt it when the man Eli called king looked at her. It was hope.

Eli heard the faint shouting and jeers before Martha did.

"King! King! King!"

Eli cried, "That's coming from Golgotha! Bubbe, I think they have crucified the king!"

He started running.

"Eli, that hill is no place for a child. You will never unsee what you see there. Return to me at once!"

But Eli ignored her, and her old legs could not keep up with those of a seven-year-old.

As they got closer, they could hear the words of the crowd: "He said he was the king. Let him come down from the cross. We'll believe him then."

"Look at him! He saved others, but he cannot save himself!"

"If you really are the king of the Jews, save yourself!"

By the time Bubbe reached the top of the hill, she found a cluster of sobbing women comforting her little grandson who lay in a heap on the ground.

She reached down and touched him. "Eli, come. We must leave this terrible place."

The stench of blood and sweat was making her sick, and the laughter from those close to the three crosses sounded like a chorus of devils.

Eli jumped to his feet. Sobbing, he pointed at the middle cross.

"Look, Bubbe. Look what they did to our king!"

Unwillingly, she looked at a man who no longer seemed human; his flesh was so torn and beaten. A crown of thorns had been pushed deep into his head. Huge spikes pinned his hands to the cross, and to get a single breath of air he had to push up with his feet that had also been nailed to the wood. She had never imagined such a nightmare of suffering.

"Eli, that man looks nothing like the king you saw on the donkey. Perhaps he is another man. They only crucify criminals."

"Bubbe, look at the sign!"

She read the sign nailed above the man's head: Jesus of Nazareth, King of the Jews.

"Eli, surely he is someone else."

One of the crying women who had been comforting Eli gently touched her arm.

"The lad is not mistaken. They have rejected and crucified their Messiah. I know it is Him; He is my son."

"Your son?"

She looked into the woman's eyes.

"Yes, my son, and the Son of God."

Bubbe's head swam. She could not have heard those words. She looked around for Eli. She heard more laughter at the foot of the cross where Roman soldiers surrounded a small lad who was shouting at them.

Heart sinking, Martha hobbled as quickly as she could toward the boy.

"You Roman swine! You are killing the best man who ever lived. I hate you! When I grow up, I will find you, and I will kill you."

The soldiers shoved him back and forth between them like he was a toy, laughing and mocking.

"Oh, we tremble with fear, you small Jewish zealot. Do you want to end up like this man, your king?"

The tallest soldier picked him up and held him high over his head so he could see the face of Jesus.

Then, the soldier threw Eli to the ground. Not going into battle, the man wore no greaves to protect his legs. Furious, Eli wrapped his arms around a leg and bit until blood filled his mouth.

"Why, you little son of Neptune!"

He shook Eli loose and drew back his foot to kick him in the head with murderous force, but two things happened.

Bubbe threw herself at the soldier, holding him, and begging, "Please, no. He is but a lad."

And a voice strong and sweet came from the middle cross, "Father, forgive them. They know not what they do."

The soldier gently disentangled the old woman and said, "Take the lad home."

Then that soldier stepped back, stared long at the middle cross, and thumped his heart once with his fist.

AND THEN CAME SUNDAY—ELI PART THREE
APRIL 2021

Should she find a physician? The boy refused to eat, drink, or sleep. He'd sat in that corner since Friday afternoon, more than twenty-four hours now, not crying, not speaking, staring straight ahead. Sometimes, he banged his head into the wall over and over until she thought he'd damage his brain, if he had any left after that terrible sight he'd seen of his king, the man he loved, beaten, tortured, and dying on a cross. It was enough to drive a grown man mad, let alone a seven-year-old boy.

Martha tried to comfort him by telling him what she had heard.

"Eli, his brave friends, Joseph and Nicodemus took his body from the cross and put it in Joseph's new tomb in a beautiful garden. They wrapped it in linen with seventy-five pounds of costly myrrh and aloes that Nicodemus bought. Seventy-five pounds, Eli! Normal burials use five pounds; only royal burials use seventy-five. Perhaps Nicodemus agrees with you that your Jesus of Nazareth was a king."

The boy moaned and started banging his head into the wall again.

"Eli, please, stop that and listen. They rolled a huge stone in front of the tomb so no grave robbers or wild animals could get inside!"

Eli made an animal-like sound himself and banged his head more furiously.

What could she do? Martha felt like banging her head into a wall herself. She had tried everything, offering Eli his favorite foods, telling him stories he usually loved, singing him psalms. Nothing worked.

I don't think the child even sees me, and I shudder to think what he is seeing.

When it came time to sleep, Eli did as he had done Friday night, sat in the corner, knees up to his chin, arms wrapped around his legs, and refused to move. She and the ancient one went to their mats, but she doubted either of them would sleep any better than they had the night before.

Hours passed, and Eli did not make a sound. At least the head banging had stopped. Could he be sleeping?

She almost jumped when the ancient one recited a phrase from a psalm: "He gives his beloved sleep."

Shocked, she heard Eli stumble toward the ancient one's sleeping mat. She could picture him curled up next to his great-grandfather, seeking comfort. Eli said nothing, but finally the tears came, man-sized sobs, terrible to hear from such a small child.

"I know, boy. I know," the quavering voice of the ancient one said. "Let it out."

It seemed Eli would never stop sobbing. Martha too had a psalm.

She cried it aloud as a prayer: "Weeping may last for the night, but joy comes in the morning."

Before sunrise, Martha felt Eli shaking her.

"It is almost morning, Bubbe. What joy? What joy is coming today?"

Now what do I say? I don't want him going back to that corner again.

"Go back to sleep, Eli. It is not morning yet."

"No." His voice was stubborn. "There is something I must do, Bubbe. I am going to the garden tomb."

"What do you intend to do there? Do you know the Roman soldiers are guarding that tomb? Will you provoke them again? You barely escaped with your life the last time!"

"No, I do not know why, but I am not angry with the soldiers anymore. But I must go to the garden tomb. You stay here with the ancient one. I will be fine. I am almost a man now, Bubbe."

She agreed that sadly the last few days had advanced him toward manhood far quicker than she would have wished, but he was far from grown.

"We will go together. Quiet, now; do not wake the ancient one."

The sky was getting lighter as they neared the garden. She could see Eli's matted hair and tear-streaked face now, and she felt a physical pain in her heart.

"What is it you need to do here, Eli?"

But the boy was once again silent.

Martha had never in all her years seen such a garden. The sun just lifting over the hills shined through flowers that reflected the colors of heaven. The air smelled sweeter than a dream.

Eli shrugged out of his little white coat and ran toward the tomb.

Where does he think he is going? If those soldiers see him...

But there were no soldiers. Eli looked at her and pointed at the huge stone rolled back from the tomb's entrance.

"Eli, do not go in there!"

"But that is why I came, Bubbe. I want to cover the feet of the king with my coat, so he won't be cold."

"Eli El-Bethel, Martha El-Bethel, come to me, my children."

Stunned, Martha looked at the man sitting on the garden bench. He held out his arms, and she saw nail prints in his palms. How could this be?

She remembered Mary's words: "He is my son, and the Son of God."

She hesitated, but Eli ran into the man's arms. Both the man and the boy were laughing and crying tears of joy.

"King, why did you let them nail you to that cross?"

"I died for a greater kingdom than you can imagine. I died for the sin of every person ever born or ever yet to be born. I took sin into my heart, there on the cross, accepted its punishment, and made it not to be. Do you believe me, Eli?"

"It is true, then?" Martha asked. "You are the Son of God?"

"Yes," Jesus smiled. "Come to set you free and make you new, just as you prayed, Martha El-Bethel. Do you believe me?"

The old one and the child both became new that day.

"Go now," Jesus said to Eli, "and be a strong soldier in my kingdom. You have a weapon so strong nothing can stand against it."

"I do?"

Jesus smiled at him. "You have love. You will live love, and you will teach love. Your Bubbe will be your first pupil."

Eli clung to him. "I do not want to leave You."

"I will be with you always, but we both have our work to do now."

Eli and his grandmother turned to leave.

"Aren't you forgetting something?" Jesus held out His arm, and Eli laid his little white coat across it.

Jesus touched the coat gently. "Thank you, my son."

He looked deeply into Martha's eyes.

"I will," she promised.

"You will what, Bubbe?" Eli asked.

But she just smiled.

That night, after Eli and the ancient one were sleeping, Martha began making two coats, a little one for Eli, and a bigger one to help the ancient one feel warm and loved. For the first time in her life, Martha El-Bethel felt warm, loved, and not alone.

She remembered the King's words: "I will be with you always."

It was true. He was with her, in her heart, smiling with her at each loving movement she made.

THAT'S A SHORT NUMBER
APRIL 2021

Our adorable four-year-old granddaughter, Ruby, hurried to meet John and me as we carried our chairs to the bonfire. She glanced back at our car and asked about missing family members. We explained why they hadn't been able to come.

Ruby looked at the people already gathered in the yard and asked, "Is this all that's coming?"

We nodded.

"Well, that's a short number." Ruby thought for a minute and added, "But if we all end up going inside, it won't feel like a short number!"

We laughed. No, Ruby, if we had ended up inside the seven adults and five kids would have felt like a much longer number.

I've been grinning about that "short number" all week, ever since last Monday night's wonderful meal and bonfire at our son and daughter-in-law's house. They agreed to wear masks, even outside, so I could come.

"We'll wear hazmat suits if we have to, to see you," our son, Dan, said.

My oncology team, because of Covid and cancer, only allows me to have limited contact with people, even family, and everyone has to wear masks. And I used to think my mother was strict!

You don't even want to hear my list of restrictions, but I'll say this. In my world, the inside of churches, stores, and restaurants no longer exists, and I miss my friends so much I feel a physical ache.

My body also imposes its own restrictions on me.

You're going to clean, cook, converse, write, read, watch a movie, and make phone calls today? Good luck with that! Have fun staying awake!

And then I sleep another twenty hour stretch and hope for a Rip Van Winkle reprieve the next day.

If I let myself think that way, life could feel like a "short number" right now. But it isn't. It's still a long number.

Have you noticed how many things are a matter of perspective? I know the optimism thing can get a bit ridiculous, like one of my favorite jokes. Before I share it, I must digress.

I was telling family my memorial service wishes the other day, for two months from now or twenty years later down these rambling backroads.

"I don't want a traditional funeral, only a memorial service. Maybe there could be coffee and donuts on the back table at church, like there used to be at the church services I loved so much. Sing lots of songs about heaven. No long sermon, just have someone talk about how to know Jesus. John, I don't want you to feel you have to do it; it might be too hard. I'd love to have our church board members oversee my memorial service. I love them, and they know and love me. Do you think they'd do it?"

John hugged me. "You could ask them."

"They can say whatever they want, and anyone else there can too. Maybe someone can tell my favorite jokes."

"Mom! Your favorite jokes?" Kimmee looked startled.

Now I'll stop digressing and tell you my favorite optimist joke. An optimist fell out of a nineteenth story window.

As he passed the ninth-floor window, on the way to the ground, people heard him shouting, "So far, so good!"

We laugh at that joke. We laugh because it's ridiculous, absurd, and wonderful.

Life might look like a short number for me right now, but I'm still shouting, "So far, so good!"

I'm blessed with a super abundance of caring family and friends who pray for me and help me through every day.

The bonfire was perfect. I sat there watching the leaping flames, loving the faces of our family, hearing the kids laughing and playing on the lighted trail in the woods, and feeling the warmth of the fire on my face. I wanted to stay forever because I knew what we should all remember; every time may be the last time, and life is too short for anything but love.

We had to say goodbye and go our separate ways, but we have the blessing of that memory to cherish forever, and we have something even more precious than that.

When John Wesley, the great circuit riding preacher was dying, he said, "Best of all, God is with us."

Because God is with us, life is never a short number.

GO TO YOUR ROOM
APRIL 2021

"Go to your room. Stay there. Don't let anyone in. Don't come out. Don't walk in your yard. Don't go to parks."

I'm under house arrest without the ankle monitor!

Mom often sent me to my room but never without a spanking first. Back in the day, there was no cut off age for spankings. Moms didn't seem to realize if spankings hadn't worked by a certain age, they weren't likely to work at all. So, if you were a member of my family, you got spanked right up to high school graduation.

I knew a man who was engaged when his dad ordered him to lie over the hood of the car. He did as he was told; the dad took off his belt and gave his son what he thought he deserved.

We may shudder now, but that was not all that uncommon back in the day.

I never told Mom how much I loved being sent to my room. Blessed peace and quietness, not to mention I had a book somewhere in there, often under my pillow. And even if Mom ordered me not to read, I did anyway. I had a conscience as a child, but it wasn't terribly active.

Alone in my room, I could lose myself in *Five Little Peppers and How They Grew*, a world where the mom struggled to provide for her five beloved children and never used a belt on any of them.

Or, I could be Jo in *Little Women*, the outspoken tomboy who loved to write. Her mother didn't spank her or her three sisters. They called her Marmee. I thought my three sisters and I could use a mother more like that. I managed to ignore the fact the children in my book world behaved much better than I did in my real world and weren't driving their Marmee crazy.

Despite the frequent spankings, I loved my real world every bit as much as my book world. I had many wonderful adventures growing up, and not all of them were against the rules!

I still love retreating to my room to read, write, or watch a movie. "Go to your room!" isn't a punishment for me, but it has been a few years since I've heard it, like maybe fifty-five? So, I chuckled when I read it in my patient portal.

"Go to your room. Stay there. Don't let anyone in. Don't come out. Tell someone to slide food under your door. Don't walk in your yard. Don't go to parks."

That may be a loose translation.

After yesterday's bone marrow biopsy and Covid test, the doctors want me to isolate so I'm healthy for tomorrow's bronchoscopy when they will go into my lungs and grab pieces of Morticia for study purposes. They can only take a few small pieces of her for this biopsy, but who knows? Maybe they'll get her heart, and it will be a fatal wound. Won't miss you a bit, Mortish!

Immediately after the lung biopsy, I'll have a PET scan. They scheduled a brain CT for Friday. As you may have guessed, I'm in the process of qualifying for the clinical trial.

The trial will involve 130 people in the United States and Europe including five from University of Michigan Hospital.

You want the big medical terms for the clinical trial? No? Skip this paragraph. It's an "open-label trial to assess the safety and preliminary efficacy of Epcoritamab in combination with other agents in subjects with B cell non-Hodgkin's Lymphoma."

Picture Epcoritamab as having two strong arms; it grabs a T-cell with one and a cancer cell with the other and hauls them close together.

Then the T-cell says, "Ah ha! I see you now, oh my enemy, you lurking, no-good scoundrel! So, your name is Morticia? Prepare to die!"

And the fight is on.

The trial lasts a year, and I will need to visit the hospital so many times I'm going to love going to my room at home. John says he loves driving Miss Donna, but he's going to appreciate crashing in our room too.

Sometimes I wonder what heaven's rooms are like. Do you?

John 14:2 says, "In my Father's house there are many mansions." Other translations say, "many rooms."

Will we each have our own room? I doubt we'll feel the need to retreat from each other the way we do here, but there is something special about a place of one's own to reflect, to read, to create.

I think we'll each have our own rooms and be free to go there whenever we want. Perhaps we'll visit each other's rooms, unless the "No Visitors, Please," sign is out.

I'll find Mom's room and tell her how much I love her and how grateful I am for all the times she said, "Go to your room!"

THE MAGICAL MONTH
APRIL 2021

Miracles happen every day especially in the month of May.

When I was a child, we folded triangular pieces of construction paper into cones at school to make May baskets. We'd fill them with flowers we found on the way home. We were delighted to discover violets but were even happy with dandelions. We'd hang a basket on a doorknob, often our own, knock or ring a bell, then run, hide, and watch to see the happy reaction the gift brought. Bless moms and grandmas everywhere for expressing joy over dandelions.

We moved from southern New York State to the northern part after I finished fourth grade. Those were my happiest childhood years, but spring crept slowly into that snowbelt land. There was never even a dandelion in sight on May first, so we made no May baskets.

I do remember a teacher constructed a beautiful maypole for us with colored streamers. We sang a song to welcome spring and "danced" around the maypole, weaving the streamers together. It was like side-stepping into another world, squinting up into the blue sunlit sky and watching those streamers weave together; I caught my breath at the magical beauty of being part of it.

It was great fun until my mother, who opposed dancing in all its forms, found out about it. She insisted not only was a maypole wrong because it included dancing, but it was a pagan tradition, and I, who had been often forbidden to dance at school, knew better.

I suppose I did know better, but I didn't regret it, even after Mom's punishment. I was an incorrigible child who seldom repented of a "crime" if there had been any fun involved. And that maypole had been more than fun; it had been a miracle of celebration and community I felt but only vaguely understood at the time.

Isn't May a month of miracles? Though our late April snow and freeze killed the bleeding heart plants, we're welcoming May with lilacs dancing and weaving for joy. The lily of the valley, our ground cover, will bloom with abandon this month too, as will many other perennials. If children on our backroads want to fill May baskets, they have many flowers to choose from. Yesterday, we passed a field that looked like someone had planted dandelions; it was acres of sunshine.

Sunshine, fresh air, family, friendships old and new, the fragrance of flowers and freshly cut grass are all gifts to me, new from the hand of God who, miracle of miracles, loves even me, His sometimes still incorrigible child.

I don't like every event of my life, but my Lord, with loving, nail-pierced hands, weaves them together like streamers on a maypole, and when I squint up into the blue, sunlit sky, I catch my breath at the magical beauty of what I see. However, each individual streamer may not be lovely on its own; some are quite dark.

A college friend died of cancer this past year.

As he fought his cancer, he told his family, "Now is the time to practice our theology."

Now John and I say that to each other.

My cancer is a bitter life ingredient, and we don't like how it tastes, but do we still believe God is good and loving? That's our theology, isn't it? Yes, we do believe it, despite fluctuating daily feelings, because we long ago learned to judge God's love by one thing only: the cross. It was there He proved His love for us. It was there He took our sins into His heart, felt the guilt and shame of each one, and suffered and died for us. And then came another miracle; He rose again.

I know Easter didn't happen in May, but each year, May seems like a resurrection of joy to me. I'm glad I'm here to see it, to rejoice in its beauty, and to celebrate its hope, its many miracles. I'm glad for the miracle of the support and love of community. We're here to walk, to dance each other Home, to weave our maypole streamers together into something better than ourselves.

I'm expecting a personal miracle any day now. After a week of less than fun tests that aren't on anyone's bucket list, I'm hoping to hear I'm accepted into a clinical drug trial at University of Michigan Hospital. They've already set up an appointment for me to get my first dose of the drug on Tuesday. We're just waiting for the drug company's final approval.

So what if my balance is off and somedays my walk looks more like a stumble? Does anyone know where there's a maypole? Point me to it; I'll dance! Do you want to meet me there? And Mom, now in heaven and probably dancing for joy herself, will understand.

UNTIL THE LAST EMBER
MAY 2021

A few blocks from the hospital, the busy traffic narrowed into one lane. The huge Cat machine in the other lane hit the road pavement repeatedly with earsplitting noise, breaking it into huge chunks, scooping them into its bucket, raising them high, and dumping them with satisfyingly loud thumps into a waiting semi.

She watched, fascinated, as the Cat yanked up a big piece of road and dumped it.

"Look! It got Morticia! She's gone."

He laughed and kept driving.

She prayed in her heart the rest of the way to the hospital: "Make it so, Lord. Let this treatment be the one that works. Yank Morticia out and dump her in a semi somewhere. But I'll love and bless You either way."

She'd had been so sick since the last treatment. She hadn't known if she'd be able to get here today.

But God and her medical team had helped her, and here she was, a few blocks from the hospital, where there would be another chance to whisper, "Die, Morticia, die, you stubborn lung tumor."

~

THEY WERE CAMPING, the two old lovers. They agreed, silly people they were, they much preferred camping in Old Bertha, their 1988 fifth wheel with her perpetual problems, to a cruise, or a trip to Cancun or Hawaii. Not that they could afford any of those camping alternatives, but even if they could, they'd still pick Bertha.

It had been a satisfying day of short hikes. They were slower on the trails now than they used to be, far slower, but with the health problems they'd both overcome, they thanked God they could still hike at all. They held hands whenever possible. Young lovers should remember life is too short not to hold hands.

They had cooked supper together over the fire in their favorite spot at Brown County State Park, a remote section where it was quiet, and they could be alone. Now they were sitting at a campfire, listening to its love language. A campfire has words for those who listen.

She was tired and started dozing in her chair.

"It's getting late, honey, do you want to go inside the camper and go to sleep?" he asked.

"Oh, please, no. Let's stay here until the last ember burns out."

And so, they did. They kept moving their chairs closer to the fire to share its last warmth, remembering old times, and dreaming new dreams. The stars came out. Finally, shivering but with hearts full of contented gratitude, they put away the camp chairs and went to bed, sleeping the deep sleep that held the promise of many tomorrows together.

"Donna, are you still doing okay?" The kind nurse smiled as he looked around the curtain.

"Thank you, Bryant. I'm fine. I guess I fell asleep. I was dreaming about camping."

"That's okay! You're here so many hours today. Sleep all you can. Can I get anything for you?"

"No thank you. I'm really fine."

And she was. Because God would be with her until the last ember burned out, hopefully after many more years of wandering down these backroads, and then a future more beautiful than any dream would begin and never end.

WHAT I SAW FROM WHERE I SAT
MAY 2021

"There once was a whaler from Pompeii,
Who went ashore to sashay,
But instead went to church,
And was forced there to perch
For a two hour long homily that went neither fore nor aft and said nothing.
The kind old whaler, probably not from Pompeii,
Wished he had gone to sashay.
Looked around church sooner.
Rig was a bark not schooner.
Its grand tonnage was packed, but most of its cargo was sleeping.
The wise old whaler, definitely not from Pompeii,
Almost left to sashay.
Knew the Cap'n wasn't heard.
Didn't even know windward.
He had no harpoon onboard, and if you aim at nothing, you hit it. Every time."
—By me, with apologies to all real poets

So, what did I see from where I sat in my hospital room last week?

Once I stopped feeling like a snail too weak to pull its hinder parts back into its shell—that's not entirely allegorical —I started thinking about harpoons. I remembered a story I'd read early in our ministry and laughed. A whaler did go to church on shore leave and listened to a homily similar to what's described above.

As the whaler tried to slip unnoticed out of church, the clergyman stopped him with a question: "What did you think of the sermon?"

Also like the poem above, the sermon had gone neither fore nor aft and said nothing, but, being a kind man, the whaler wasn't sure what to say.

Finally, he responded: "Well, matey, you said fine words, but you had no harpoon on board."

Would you believe that story has shaped John's preaching ministry and my writing? When John first graduated from college and became John Poole, BA in theology, and ThB in Bible and theology, his sermons were more informational than motivational.

When John asked me what I thought about one overly informational sermon, I asked him, "What was your harpoon, matey?"

I sometimes now regret asking that question when his sermon harpoon pokes me! And now he never gets behind the pulpit without a harpoon onboard.

The same is true in my writing. Informational writing is fine, if that's the writer's goal. What's my goal when I write? If I don't know my goal, I'm wasting my time and yours.

So, I grinned when I thought of that story in the hospital and looked around for harpoons for you and for me.

I found my first harpoon. It had "Jesus" written on it.

Sometimes, I forget Jesus is the hub of the wheel of my life.

I promise I'm not digressing, but John and I saw a twelve-year old on the news who'd graduated from high school and college at the same time. He's quite the goal-driven kid.

I said to John, "When I was twelve my goal was to get my cards to stay on the spokes of my bike with clip clothespins because they made the coolest sound."

Obviously, I was not like the goal-driven kid on the news.

I loved riding my bike. But what if the hub of my bike had been off-center so some spokes were longer and some shorter? You can imagine how well that wheel would have gone around!

When I make Jesus my focus, He keeps my spokes, the other things in my life, more even. I don't mean my life is easy or perfect. I mean the Lord keeps things more balanced.

So, I try to keep the main thing, Jesus, the main thing. He's my hub.

Many other things also matter dearly to me: family, church family, friends, my writing, my readers, finding joy, and so much more. These things are my "harpoons" in life, my goals. Cancer is my great reminder that I don't have earth-time forever, and now is when I better polish up my harpoons and avoid getting sidetracked by the million and one things that don't matter.

But here's something else I see from where I sit in the hospital room. I see a harpoon with your name on it, because if you read what I write, you matter to me. This harpoon may be the most important thing I ever send your way, because it will prepare you for this life and for eternity.

Next to your name, the harpoon has the name Jesus and John 3:16:

"For God so loved the world, that he gave his only

begotten Son, that whosoever believeth in him should not perish, but have everlasting life."

Notice it doesn't say you get eternal life by being a good person, or being a good Catholic, or being Baptist. It says believe in Jesus, to stake your eternity on Who He is and all He did for you.

There are only two names on that harpoon, your name and His. Those two are more than enough for here and for forever. And that's what I saw from where I sat.

OH, WHAT A WONDERFUL GIFT
JUNE 2021

The little girl had a perfectly heart shaped face, long, dark brown braids, and almost black eyes. She watched, brown eyes dancing with excitement, while I opened my Christmas gift from her, one she'd saved pennies, nickels, and dimes to buy me. I was a year older, her big sister, and she knew I wanted gold, doll-sized silverware.

There it was in my hands, the silverware I'd longed for but never really expected to have. I looked at her happy smile, and then I did something so unbelievably cruel tears still sting my eyes when I remember. We'd been fighting, some little girl sister argument over something now long forgotten.

"I don't want this stupid stuff," I said to Mary. "You keep it."

She didn't say a word, but her face. Oh, that sweet face. Her lips trembled. Tears spilled out of those dark eyes and ran down her cheeks. I did love the gift. I was sorry for the words the moment I said them. It was a lesson it would take me a lifetime to learn; there is no taking back cruel words once said.

Mom snatched the gift from my hands and gave it to Mary.

"Donna, you will never touch these as long as you live," Mom said. "Do you hear me? Never."

And I never did.

Many years later, I finally apologized, and Mary forgave me, but the memory lingers of a wonderful gift rejected and the sweet giver deeply hurt.

∼

OFTEN THESE DAYS, because I'm so sick, I find myself once again unappreciative of a gift, the gift of life. I'm in a treatment cycle right now. I get GemOx chemotherapy and a trial drug on Tuesday. From Thursday through Monday afternoon, I'm too sick to appreciate much of anything; I just survive. But by late Monday afternoon I start to rejoin the land of the living barely in time to drag myself back to the hospital, but this time, I'm not dreading the appointment as much. See, every other Tuesday, I get a bit of a reprieve. I get only the trial drug, no chemotherapy. Without the chemotherapy, I don't feel nearly as sick. God wipes a film from my eyes and once again I see and appreciate the wonder of life.

Remember being a kid, swinging high, lying back in the swing, and looking at life from upside down? Breathtaking, wasn't it? It's like that when I once again see.

In the hospital parking lot, I reach for John's hand, and he smiles at me. I love how boyish his smile still is, and the way he jokes about driving Miss Donna and never complains about the many hours he spends in the car. I think about how lovely my care team is: doctors, nurses, the lady who schedules everything, and the phlebotomists—especially the one who finds me every week, no matter where I am, and gives me a Bible verse to help me through the day. I picture home and know it will be spotless when I get there, because our daughter, Kimmee, not only cooks gourmet meals, but she also cleans, gardens, and does a hundred other things.

We pull out of the hospital parking lot and ease our way into traffic. I grin at how young the pedestrian traffic is; it's mostly students and hospital employees riding bikes, walking fast, jogging, or running, some with ponytails swinging side to side.

Live, kids, live! The world needs your youth, your energy, your enthusiasm.

When we get out of the city, I catch my breath at the beauty of nature's bounty. It has rained, and June is green with hope. So many different shades of green combine to make one glorious watercolor wash. Flowers brighten the landscape. I'm a tree hugger from way back. If I only had the energy, I'd ask John to stop the car so I could get out and throw my arms around the rough bark of one and feel glad for its Creator.

I'll feel better for a few days now until it's time for chemo again next Tuesday.

Last Sunday, I curled up in bed barely alert, only awake enough to know I was sicker than a dog. This Sunday, Kimmee will take me to parking lot church. I might even put my hand over my heart and try to sing if I don't run out of breath. I know I'll cry; I seldom make it through a parking lot church service without grateful tears. And Kimmee won't laugh or roll her eyes. She'll just hug me or touch my arm and ask if I'm okay.

Later on Sunday, we'll finally celebrate a late Easter with our kids and grandkids. We'll watch the grandkids hunt for eggs in the grass at our son and daughter in law's house and give them their Easter baskets. We'll take off our masks long enough to eat together. Our son or daughter-in-law will probably build a fire, and we'll sit around it and laugh and talk and love every minute together until the last ember.

Can we ever cherish the gift of life too much? If we take it for granted, if we let our trials rub off the shine until only the gray remains, are we throwing the gift back at its Creator?

"I don't want this stupid stuff. You keep it."

In our sicker than a dog days, we may be incapable of loving life; everyone has those survival mode times. But when we can, let's hug the people we love and the trees too; let's laugh and sing and put our hands over our hearts and cry. Because life is good. Oh, what a wonderful gift!

SONGS IN THE NIGHT
JUNE 2021

"In a real dark night of the soul it is always three o'clock in the morning." –F. Scott Fitzgerald

The old mystics used to talk about the dark night of the soul, and singers and poets ever since have adapted the phrase for their own meaning.

When it's dark inside, do we forget to sing? We may. Friends can help us then.

"A friend hears the song in my heart and sings it back to me when I've forgotten the words." –Unknown

God gives songs in the night, Job 35:10. John and I used to listen to a radio program titled *Songs in the Night* on Sunday nights after we put our young children to bed. Many years later, our sons told us as soon as they heard the theme music play, they covered their heads with their blankets. They were little boys and thought the program's title was **Sounds** *in the Night*. They didn't want to hear any scary sounds in the night!

God gave me songs this week. A friend, Boyd Allen, visited our church on Sunday, played his guitar, and sang, "The Old Country Church." Perhaps it's a good thing I was listening from Kimmee's car in the parking lot instead of being inside. I used up many tissues crying at the good memories that song recalled.

On Tuesday I heard more music. Bob Huffman is a music therapist at University of Michigan Hospital. He visits oncology patients because he loves to give songs in the night. We patients getting strong chemotherapy listen to him play his guitar, tap our toes in our beds or recliners, and almost forget cancer for a while.

We're hurting; it's starting to get dark inside, but Bob hears the songs in our hearts and sings them back to us when we've forgotten the words.

I had a chance to talk to Bob on Tuesday. I asked if what I'd read was true, that music is the only activity that activates the entire brain. He said he'd read the same thing. We talked about the mysterious ability of music to recreate memories, to calm, to help alleviate pain.

"There is still so much we don't know about the power of music," he said.

He can play about any style of guitar music. I requested "Take Me Home, Country Roads."

"You mean the John Denver 'Country Roads?'"

He smiled and not only played it but sang it as well.

Bob also played "The Sound of Silence" by Simon & Garfunkel; suddenly it was 1965, and I was a junior in high school with my whole life before me. I loved music when I was a teenager.

Mom didn't like us to play music at home; looking back, I understand why. Six of us, seven when my older sister visited, lived in a trailer ten feet wide and fifty feet long.

That tin box magnified every sound, and we weren't quiet kids.

I do remember Mom singing a few hymns though, "I Come to the Garden Alone," and "God Will Take Care of You." In my memories, when Mom sang, she was always in the kitchen. Mom made wonderful spaghetti, homemade donuts, potato pies, and pasta fazool, so when I remember her music, I remember her food. I can almost smell the thick spaghetti sauce simmering on the stove.

No cussing was allowed in the home I grew up in, not even in songs. Mom had a bar of soap ready for anyone who offended the no cussing rule, but when I was a child and got mad enough at my younger sister, Mary, I sang, "Bloody Mary." She hated the words, "Bloody Mary is the girl I love," and when I shouted out the last six words including the cuss word, she told Mom, and I got to sink my teeth into the soap. So, remembering that song makes me taste soap!

Macy, our granddaughter, is a genius at remembering lyrics, and she's my hero in many ways. With a chromosome deletion and addition, her determination has taken her further than experts ever thought she would go. When Macy was preschool age, she memorized every word of every verse of every song we sang at church. She picked up the words to songs on the radio and on her CDs as well. She sang a song that named all the presidents. I often thought if someone could put everything Macy needed to know to music, she could learn it all without struggling.

What is there about music? My husband, John and I used to participate in a nursing home ministry pre the two C's—cancer and Covid. People in the home, some no longer able to speak a sentence or even tell you their names or room numbers, could still sing the words to hymns they had learned long ago.

After Bob played on Tuesday at the chemo center, I did

something I never do, unless I'm writing. I shared with him, a stranger, some of my cancer struggles. But you know what? We weren't really strangers anymore. He gave me one of his CDs to listen to at home. It's an easy listening style, *Bobby Charles Forever and a Day*. My husband and I loved it.

I hope you aren't facing that dark night of the soul where it's always three o'clock in the morning, but if you aren't, you may someday. If it happens, listen for a whisper of a song. God will give you a song in the night, even if its harmony is tears.

When God makes the new heaven and the new earth, we won't need our songs in the night; I don't know if we'll even remember them. He'll wipe away all our tears, and we'll have an eternity of joy and music!

The Best Is Yet to Be.

IT'S A NOISY WORLD ALRIGHT
JUNE 2021

Just smile and wave boys, smile and wave. That's what my kind and I do because we don't know any other proper response. We likely have no idea what you said.

I don't know how long I've been hard of hearing, probably a long while. I do know we've had a good friend for over forty-five years, and I've never heard more than half of what he's said. Maybe that's why we're such good friends!

Did you know that hard of hearing people are more likely than the general population to get early dementia? I think I know why. Without meaning to, we withdraw little by little into our own worlds and let conversation flow on around us. It's easier than asking, "What did you say?" or, "Would you repeat that?" every two minutes. We catch fragments of conversations and respond when we can.

Time passes, and we don't realize how bad our hearing loss has become. Until something out of the ordinary makes us face reality.

For me, it was not being able to hear my oncologist and many of my chemotherapy nurses. I do ask them to repeat.

Otherwise, I wouldn't know if my oncologist said, "Call in hospice," or, "Don't eat popsicles." That's a difference I might need to know!

So, John and I had the hearing aid conversation. We don't have the type of Medicare and the supplementary program that pays for hearing aids, but we don't want to switch. You wouldn't either if you were us! Our insurance has paid every cent of a brain surgery, ICU stays, other minor surgeries and hospitalizations, monthly IVIg treatments that cost about twenty-seven grand each, and all my chemotherapy. Our insurance agent told us never to change it.

Without insurance help, we were on our own to pay for whatever hearing aids we bought, so I started researching. John hates to hear this analogy, but I sometimes ask him how much money he wants to put into an old and perhaps dying horse!

I saw an ad on my phone for inexpensive hearing aids available online and asked my Facebook friends for opinions. I got lots of ideas from them, and something totally unexpected. One of God's earth angels we've known for years lives in a nearby town. He saw my Facebook post and messaged me. He had the kind of hearing aids I'd asked about in an upgraded version. He'd worn them only two weeks and decided to go with something else. The company refused to let him return them. You guessed it; he gave them to me. I wore them for the first-time last night.

We ate in the living room, as we do most nights. Not only could I hear every word said in the living room, but I could also hear conversations in the kitchen when people when back for seconds. It was amazing, and overwhelming.

I often brag about my wonderful family so I'm sorry to tell you this, but they are incredibly noisy. They toss silverware from the island into the sink, and it sounds like bombs exploding. I had to leave the kitchen. One of them has this high piercing whistle. I enjoyed it pre-hearing aids. I thought it was a quiet, tuneless whistle; at least, I could never pick out a tune. When they turn on a light switch in this old house it sounds like a cap gun going off. And their voices are so loud!

They laughed at me and said, "Wait until the whole family gets together. What are you going to do then?"

I thought about our family, all twenty-three of us, thirteen grandkids. I know what I'm going to do then. I'm not going to wear my wonderful new hearing aids. I've prayed for hearing aids for years, and I'm beyond grateful for these, but like some wise sage said, probably my mom, "There's such a thing as too much of a good thing."

LET FREEDOM RING
JULY 2021

"Ring the bells that still can ring,
forget your perfect offering.
There is a crack in everything.
That's how the light gets in." –Leonard Cohen

On Memorial Day, July Fourth, and Labor Day, I'm a sniffling, patriotic mess at our small-town parades, perhaps to the dismay of my family; though, I think they're used to me by now. From the children wobbling by on their decorated bikes, to the groups giving away water and tiny flags, to the band never in step, though usually in tune, everything makes me cry. And forget it when the VFW passes by proudly carrying our American flag. I stand with my hand over my heart, and tears run down my face. God bless America!

One long-ago parade holiday we were about ready to load the kids in the car to go to the parade when someone from church called my pastor husband and needed him to come for counseling.

"Please, hurry," the person said.

John rushed out the door and said, "I'm sorry, honey. Maybe you can get a ride to the parade with Kenneth and Mae."

I hesitated. I hated to bother the Hales, our neighbors; though, I knew they'd say it was no bother. Johnnie was only a baby and didn't know we'd planned to go to the parade, but Angie, his toddler sister knew. I looked at her face, her brown eyes begging. And I wanted to go too. I called Hales.

Kenneth and Mae were elderly, and two of the kindest people God ever made. They pulled up to our back door. I put Angie in their backseat first, told her to wrap both arms around her chunky brother until I could get in, loaded the old, impossibly heavy baby stroller in next, and climbed in last.

I took Johnnie from Angie and held him on my lap; back then baby seats weren't required or the norm.

"Thanks so much!" I said to Hales.

"It will be more fun to watch the parade with little ones!" Mae replied.

Kenneth found a perfect parking spot; the parade would go right by us as it turned the corner. The street was full of children and many of them had helium balloons. Angie noticed.

"I'm sure they are giving those away a few blocks up the street by the speaker's stand," Mae said. "You could get her one."

I hopped out of the car, told Angie to wrap both arms around her chunky brother, hauled out the impossibly heavy stroller, and struggled to unfold it. I put Johnnie in it. Angie got out, and we walked the few blocks. I could feel sweat running down my face and back. When we got there, the balloons were gone. I comforted Angie, and we began our walk back to the car.

Repeat. Open the back door. Help Angie in. Take Johnnie out of the stroller and tell Angie to wrap both arms around her chunky brother until I can get in. Fold the impossibly heavy stroller and heave it into the back seat. Climb in myself and take Johnnie.

That's when the elderly woman from the front seat spoke: "Honey, I do believe you're in the wrong car."

Was it worth it all when the band straggled by, out of step but not out of tune, and the VFW walked by carrying our American flag, and I stood with my hand over my heart and tears running down my face? Oh, it was!

It wasn't a perfect day, and we don't have a perfect country, but freedom is still ours, if we don't let it slip through our fingers. No, it's not a perfect freedom; there has never been such a thing.

Oh, wait, there is one perfect freedom offered by God to each of us. Jesus died on the cross to give us freedom from the penalty and power of sin. If we confess our sin and need of saving; He gives us that perfect freedom, and "If the Son therefore shall make you free, you shall be free indeed."[1]

Free to enjoy eternal life!

I can't remember if John was home yet when Kenneth and Mae dropped me off at the back door; I don't think he was. Angie didn't get her red balloon. I needed a shower. Johnnie needed to chill.

Our country may need a shower, more red balloons, and a time to chill. We all see what's broken in America, but today, let's celebrate what we have. I'm not always proud of America, but I'm proud to be an American. God, bless the USA! We don't deserve it, but please, God, for the sake of your praying, repenting, hoping people, do it anyway.

"Ring the bells that still can ring,
forget your perfect offering.
There is a crack in everything.
That's how the light gets in." –Leonard Cohen

GROW OLD ALONG WITH ME
JULY 2021

The bride's mother was trembling with exhaustion; it was her first outing since the stroke had paralyzed her right arm and left her right leg with a limp.

The groom's mother was choking back tears; was her baby boy really grown and married? She said when she got home from the wedding she felt like standing on the roof of the house and shouting to the world, "You can't have him. He's mine!"

But for the moment, both mothers and the rest of the guests smiled and waved goodbye to the bride and groom with calls of, "Good luck!" and "God bless you!"

The twenty-year old bride and groom drove a few miles; then he pulled over and stopped.

How romantic! she thought. *He's going to kiss me.*

"Do you have the envelope with all the money people gave us?" he asked.

She nodded.

"Let's count it!"

Money for the honeymoon was short, and he wanted to see if there would be enough.

Money throughout the years would be short. Sometimes they didn't even spend money on anniversary cards, let alone flowers, dinner, or gifts. A simple, "Happy anniversary, honey," had to do.

The twentieth anniversary is special, but the two of them had no more money than they had the day they'd married. There would be no celebration, or so they thought. They had a five-month-old baby, three older children, and a happy, simple life. That was celebration enough.

But the three older children had something else in mind. They were seventeen, fourteen and twelve, and had a little money left from birthdays and Christmas. To supplement what they had, they looked under couch cushions and in the car and found some change. Off to the grocery store they went, came back, and prepared a delicious picnic.

"Mom and Dad," one of them announced, "we're taking you to Cascades Park to celebrate your anniversary."

The weather was perfect that day, August 1, 1989, not too hot or too cold. The mom cried when she saw the beautiful picnic so lovingly prepared.

"We have a surprise, Mom. We heard you say once you wished you could go on one of the paddlewheel boats. We rented one for you and Dad. We'll push the baby in her stroller and watch you. Go have fun!"

The mom felt like a kid that half hour in the paddle wheel boat. It was even more fun than she'd imagined.

"Now you kids take the boat for a ride," the mom said, when they hauled it back to shore.

The kids looked at each other sheepishly. "We don't have enough money to rent a boat for us. We only had enough to rent it for you."

"Oh, honey!" The mom looked pleadingly at the dad. "Can we rent a boat for the kids to ride? They did all this for us!"

The dad looked miserable. "I'd love to rent a boat for the kids. But I only have fifty cents."

Someone laughed, and then they were all laughing. It was okay. It had been a wonderful day. And as sad as the mom felt not to be able to give the kids a ride on the paddle wheel boat, her gratitude for their love and sacrifice overshadowed the sorrow. They had raised loving, giving, generous children.

And the baby in the stroller? She began giving before she could talk. At church, she gave all her cheerios to the baby boy sitting in front of her. When she was a little girl, she planned special things for her parents as often as she could. She spent all her money on people she loved.

One year, their giving girl turned into a miser and refused to spend a cent on anyone or anything. Her parents were confused by this abrupt change in personality, but the mystery cleared up as August approached. She had saved every penny to send them back to spend their anniversary night where they'd spent their honeymoon. Her brother pitched in the little she lacked at the end.

Years flew by, and it was time for the mom and dad's fiftieth anniversary. The giving girl organized a beautiful party, far lovelier than her parents' wedding had been. The decorations and food were perfect.

The giving girl's husband and some of her family helped, but she worked so hard her feet swelled so she could barely get them into flip flops.

Family and friends came from near and far to celebrate with the couple and watch them renew their vows. It was a magical day, the kind you read about in storybooks but never expect to live, and the mom tried to hold every minute in her heart.

The mom and dad watched their grown kids, in-law kids, and others clean up after the party. The mom and dad helped too. By then the giving girl could barely walk, but love kept her going.

That night, the mom lay in bed with tears running down her cheeks, thinking of the beauty of the party and the story of love those swollen feet told. She thanked God for the loving, sacrificial children He'd given to them.

How rich they were in the love they shared together! It had grown so much it had burst the seams of their hearts and had flowed out to comfort the wounded and hurt people God had sent their way.

The mom hoped what Oswald Chambers had written was true of them:

> "Our love but makes a more sure haven of rest for multitudes of strained and stressed lives. From our love should spring great patience and gentleness and service for others, for love is of God."

August 1, 2021, that couple will be married for fifty-two years. He'll preach at the country church he's loved and pastored at for forty-seven years. If her chemotherapy reactions don't prevent it, she'll listen to him preach on the radio in the parking lot; her oncologist won't allow her to be in a group of people. Later, their giving girl, who has been taking wonderful care of them during this year long cancer journey, will fix them something to eat.

Before they sleep, they'll repeat their vows, and she'll say, "Grow old along with me; the best is yet to be."

Please, dear Lord, may it be true.

She'll think of their four kids, their four in-law kids, and their thirteen grandkids. She'll think of their extended family, church family, and the multitude of friends who love and pray for them. And she'll know something: they are the richest couple alive.

WHEN AUGUST LASTED FOREVER
AUGUST 2021

It was time! Mary and I left early in the morning. We wore our sweaters, because even though it was August it was cool in the foothills of the Adirondacks Mountains. We packed our lunches into brown paper bags, even though we knew we'd eat lots of the treasure we were hunting and sure to find. We set off the kind of energy only nine-and ten-year old's can claim. We had our pails and lots of enthusiasm.

We had no set hiking route; we didn't know exactly where we were going, even though this wasn't our first time climbing the foothills to look for wild blackberries. We just walked down the road until we found a field not fenced off with barbed wire or a hot wire—the worst—cut through and started the steep climb. Our younger sister, Ginny, remembers going with us once. I imagine it was a strenuous hike for her little, short legs!

It didn't take long for us to find our first row of luscious wild blackberries growing in a tangle with cat claw thorns impossible to avoid. Blackberries, raspberries, strawberries, and almonds all belong to the rose family, but we didn't know that then, and wouldn't have cared if we had. We only cared about stuffing our mouths, filling our pails, finding adventure, and finally heading home for our reward: Mom's best in the world blackberry pie.

Once we stumbled on a long-forsaken boy scout camp with its old, crumbling buildings. My imagination told me a story of a deranged killer who'd found the camp at night; now the bodies of little cub scouts and their scout master were skeletons buried beneath my feet. I made up some excuse why we shouldn't linger there.

Mary tried to teach me the art of walking silently through the woods like a native American, one foot exactly ahead of the other, making no sound. She was much better at it than I. Every time I snapped a twig, she looked back reproachfully at me with her dark eyes until we both laughed and gave up.

As the day warmed, we took off our sweaters and tied them around our waists. We rolled them and used them as pillows for naps after a picnic lunch.

We saved our lunch bags; woe to the child in our family who returned from an adventure or a day of school without a lunch bag.

I remember detesting the old, wrinkled bag at lunch time in the school cafeteria. It was sad enough not to have money to buy lunch, but couldn't we at least throw out the lunch bag each day the way the other kids who brought their lunches did? Apparently, their moms weren't in the running for the title of Most Frugal Mom USA. But then, their moms probably couldn't make the best blackberry pie in the USA either!

After lunch, we either continued exploring or picked more berries. I remember reaching into one bush to get a berry bigger than my thumb when several snakes slid over my right arm, dropped to the ground, and slithered away. It happened so fast there wasn't even time to scream.

"Did you see that? I almost got bit by three, or six, or maybe even nine rattlesnakes!"

Mary shook her head. "I didn't see any snakes. And I'm sure they were only garter snakes."

Though rattlers do live in the foothills of the Adirondacks, I later learned that it's very common for garter snakes to lurk in the berry bushes. Mice love berries; snakes love mice; you finish the equation. But in my mind back then, I was a hero, almost as brave as Nancy Drew who stood up to criminals. I stayed right where I was and kept picking berries. No two dozen rattle snakes were going to scare me away from getting blackberry pie!

As you might guess, my story of the dangerous encounter grew with the telling. I was quite disappointed when my parents, instead of admiring my sheer courage of braving rattlesnakes, agreed with Mary that the snakes had been harmless garter snakes, waiting to eat mice, with no interest in eating a sweaty fifth grade girl.

It seemed to Mary and me those carefree days of August adventure would last always. Forever we would be sisters, climbing the hills, stuffing our mouths with the sweetness of wild blackberries, sharing laughter and the scratches from thorns, and going home to parents, siblings, and the world's best blackberry pie.

WHEN DAYLIGHT FADES
AUGUST 2021

Today is the end.

How'd you like that for a dramatic opening? Okay, I know it isn't really the end of summer, but August 31 and Labor Day weekend have always seemed like summer's last hurrah to me. Not that I even noticed much of summer this year.

Ross Ellet, my favorite meteorologist, says 2021 is Toledo's second hottest summer since people began keeping records in 1873. I did notice the heat and the humidity. Our antenna TV picks up the Toledo stations and "tropical" is a word we heard used often to describe the weather this summer.

I felt the heat as I staggered from house to car to go for my chemo treatments. We saw the haze hover over corn and bean fields as we traveled. I remembered how the blacktop used to bubble and stick to my flipflops on hot days when I was a girl and wondered if the roads were the same now, but I was too tired to ask John. He drove me to my treatments and understood when I was too tired to talk. I felt bad about the wasted conversation time, but we held hands sometimes, and we were together.

If I were a child going back to school and the teacher asked how I'd spent my summer, I'd say, "Getting chemotherapy, being sicker than the proverbial dog, and sleeping."

If you've been rambling this bumpy backroad with me, you know I have a refractory cancer, resistant to treatment. Morticia, my lung tumor, ate R-CHOP chemo for lunch and grew. She stubbornly survived radiation and GemOx chemo. John and I decided no more chemo once GemOx finished, and my oncologist agreed. So, after fourteen chemo treatments and eleven radiation sessions Morticia still lives.

But I'm remaining in the drug trial for Epcoritamab, and it's helping. Recent scans showed Morticia shrunk a bit, and perhaps my upcoming ones will show she has shrieked and melted like the Wicked Witch of the West!

With my last chemo a few weeks behind me, my brain is starting to wake. I notice the shorter days and feel sad. I don't love summer's extreme heat, but I do love long days filled with light. Ross Ellet says our next 7:00 a.m. sunrise won't be until March 7, 2022. We're losing three minutes of daylight every day.

I chase that daylight in my imagination and beg it to return. One of my favorite verses, Proverbs 4:18, says,

> "The path of the just is as the shining light, that shineth more and more unto the perfect day."

The Berean Study Bible puts it this way, "The path of the righteous is like the first gleam of dawn, shining brighter and brighter until midday."

When daylight fades from our view it's getting light on the other side of the world. The sun is always shining somewhere, and when God trusts us to walk in the dark, we can be sure He's holding our hands. It's interesting, I think, that there won't be any darkness in heaven.

> "And there shall be no night there; and they need no candle, neither light of the sun; for the Lord God giveth them light: and they shall reign for ever and ever." –Revelation 22:5

Until heaven comes, we'll face times of darkness, of suffering, of loss, times when daylight fades. It helps then, I think, to turn our faces to the light we have, however dim.

It doesn't take much light to brighten the darkness. That's why I love the little electric candles in the windows of our old farmhouse. It's why that commercial was such a success, "We'll leave the light on for you." We're drawn to light.

Tom Bodett was an NPR personality when Motel 6 hired him in 1986 to be the voice for their commercials. He ad-libbed the line, "We'll leave the light on for you," while recording his first commercial. It became an instant and lasting success for over a quarter of a century. It won many awards. *Advertising Age Magazine* named it one of the one-hundred best ads of the twentieth century.

God always leaves a light on for us. When we turn our faces to God, we reflect His light, and we can leave the light on for others who are hurting and feeling alone in the darkness. I can't think of a better reason for still being here and not over there where the daylight never fades.

DANCE OF THE BUTTERFLIES
SEPTEMBER 2021

I'm standing in a country field in a comforting September silence, alone except for the thousands, perhaps millions of butterflies dancing with delight over the wildflowers.

My memories are fading fast along with the shrieking sounds of collapsing metal and screams for help. I remember the horrified looks of my fellow firefighters when we realized the thuds we were hearing were bodies, bodies hitting the canopy. People were jumping to their deaths?

I looked up at the twisted building torn almost in two by the plane, and I ran for the stairs. I had to help people get out.

I prayed as my feet pounded the steps, prayed for my wife and babies at home, prayed for my own safety, prayed God would help me rescue some from this burning hell. Smoke seared my lungs and blinded my eyes, but I did save a few before pain, unbearable crushing pain unlike anything I'd ever imagined in my thirty-two years tore through my body. I must have passed out.

This quiet field, is it a dream? I hold out my hand, and a

butterfly lands on it. I feel its tiny feet before it flies away to rejoin the dance.

I breathe deeply, the sweetest air I've ever known. My eyes are clear, no longer crying black, smoke-filled tears. Running through the field toward me I see people I've loved, my parents, my grandparents, my childhood Sunday school teacher, so many family members and friends. I'm enveloped in love, and the butterflies dance around us.

Suddenly, the butterflies hover midflight, unmoving. My dear ones stop their shouts of rejoicing and fall to their faces. So do I. There they are, the Father and the Son. Where is the Holy Spirit? Oh, I know. He fills my heart so completely there is nothing left but love, and I weep tears of joy.

The Son lifts me up, and I look into His face—Jesus, the One I've loved so long. I kiss the nail print in His hand.

"Thank you, my Savior, for taking my sin into Your heart when You suffered on the cross, for taking my punishment, and making my sin no longer exist. Why, why did You do it?"

He throws back His head and laughs, and the melody fills the heavens.

"I did it for love. Love is the reason for everything."

The Father stretches out His arms, holds me to His chest, and I feel the pulsing heart of the universe. With every beat it says, "love, love, love."

I pull back, struggling to remember the smoke, the screams, the suffering, the stench of death.

"But why did that have to happen?" I ask.

"Love is not the law of earth yet," the Father says. "But it will be someday. Will you help me with that?"

The Lord Jesus takes my hand, holds it high, and says, "Of course he will help. He has already begun. Greater love has no man than this, that a man lay down his life for his friends."

Now millions take up the chant, "Greater love has no man than this, that a man lay down his life for his friends."

But they aren't looking at me. They are looking at Jesus, God the Son.

"Lord," I whisper to Him, "what's the date?"

He smiles. "Do you mean in earth time?"

I nod.

"September 11, 2021."

"What? 2021? But didn't I get here only a minute ago on September 11, 2001?"

He laughs again, that beautiful sound. I can't help but join, and so do millions upon millions of others.

"Yes," He says. "It was just a minute ago heaven time."

We're standing on a bit of a hill; I can overlook the crowd and see the field with the butterflies. Still they dance.

A REAL WINNER
SEPTEMBER 2021

It was a beautiful autumn day, perfect for cross country. We stood in the crowd cheering on the exhausted runners as they raced to the finish line. Megan, our granddaughter, was in the first group, blonde ponytail swinging side to side, running like a deer, her graceful stride making the long race look so much easier than it was. We hollered her name until we were hoarse, and Megan finished well, earning another PR and winning a medal.

On that long ago autumn day, we waited for Megan to cool down from her run, talk to her coach, and get congratulations from her teammates. When it was our turn, we hugged her and told her how proud we were.

By then the cross country teams were gathering under their schools' brightly colored canopies, packing gear, and getting ready to board buses. Spectators drifted away from the sidelines and walked to their cars. We said goodbye to other family members and turned to head to our vehicle.

Then I saw something almost unbelievable.

"Wait! John, look!"

He followed my glance down the track. A lone runner was still coming in, so late, so far behind all the others. Her weary feet pounded the track slowly, but she kept coming. I searched her face for signs of sorrow or embarrassment, but all I saw was a spunky determination to finish what she'd started.

You go, girl! You run! You're a real winner!

Now Reece, our grandson, runs for that same school Megan graduated from many years ago, and he too runs fast and finishes well. Years have passed since that perfect autumn day. I don't remember Megan's time now, or where she placed; though, I was proud of it then. But I remember that determined girl running so slowly, almost at walking speed, but finishing what she started.

I wonder what became her. Did she go on to college or get a job? I have a hunch whatever she did or will do in life it won't involve quitting.

We don't always get to meander backcountry roads in beautiful sunshine on perfect autumn days when life is easy for the living. Sometimes hard, heartbreaking circumstances force us to push through cold rainstorms, slosh through mud, and keep going even when we've already spent our ounce of strength five miles earlier.

It would be so easy then, wouldn't it, to curl up and give in, to let our tears mingle with the cold rain and call it quits?

"It's always too soon to quit." –Warren W. Wiersbe

God says when we're weak we're strong—strong in the strength He gives us. We can pound the track with weary feet, even when we're so far behind the others no one sees us on the track.

God Himself and an unseen heavenly host cheer for us.

"Keep going! Keep putting one foot ahead of the other!"

And so, we do. We run; we walk, and we crawl until hands and knees bleed. We may not see the other runners, but we gain courage knowing they too are giving their best. We're not alone; we're walking each other Home with our love and prayers.

When weary and bedraggled we finally reach the finish line, God will greet us with a smile, a hug, and the words, "Well done! Well done, my good and faithful servants."

Heaven's halls will echo with cheers of joyful celebration, and we'll be so glad then we didn't quit!

AN UNEXPECTED TRIO
SEPTEMBER 2021

We were an unlikely trio, two women and a man, separated by many miles. One lived in Iowa, one in Michigan, and one in South Carolina. We began our song in May/June of 2020, a melody of non-Hodgkin's lymphoma, sung in three-part harmony. When I prayed for one of us, I prayed for three of us.

Non-Hodgkin's lymphoma (NHL) has a mind of its own and goes where it will go. Irv's settled in his brain; Debbie's went to her pancreas, and mine made itself at home in my abdomen and lung.

We went to college with Irv and hadn't seen him since, but we followed him on Facebook. Irv earned degrees from Clarks Summit University, Bob Jones University, and the University of Cincinnati Conservatory of Music, and he had incredible, God-given musical talent. He became a college professor at three different colleges and was a minister of music at four churches. His passion in life was Soli Deo Gloria—Glory to God alone.

When Irv found out NHL had invaded his brain, he

commented to loved ones, "Now is the time to practice our theology."

Irv didn't whimper or whine or ask, "Why me?" His life sang praise to God alone for all the short but brutal days of his cancer journey.

Irv's daughter wrote in a social media post, "June 2020 was the beginning. November 2020 was the end. 143 days fell in between."

Then our trio became a duet. Debbie, a pastor's wife beloved by her family and her church family, was still fighting. In May of 2020, Debbie had received her cancer diagnosis in the emergency room.

She wrote, "God was in control—I knew that. I determined there in the ER that I would be a grateful, thankful patient, and trust God with everything."

Her battle was hard; the side effects of the treatments were almost unbearable. But Debbie didn't whimper or whine or ask why me; though, I'm sure she sometimes sobbed in pain. For all the days of her treatment, Debbie wanted the same thing Irv wanted, Soli Deo Gloria.

Finally, Debbie heard the wonderful news that she was cancer free. Through all the difficult days of chemotherapy and still today, Debbie's life sings praises to God alone.

In May of 2020, I started wheezing, a funny noise that made me laugh. I thought it was my myasthenia gravis. Kimmee, our daughter, wasn't laughing. Concerned I might have pneumonia, she insisted I call our family doctor. Within days, I had my cancer diagnosis. At first the doctors thought it was small cell lung cancer, but a biopsy showed it was NHL, a cancer that usually responds well to treatment.

The key word is *usually*. If you've been walking these hilly backroads with me long, you know Morticia, my lung tumor, is stubborn and resistant to treatment. So far, she has survived six treatments of R-CHOP chemotherapy, eight of GemOx chemotherapy, and eleven of radiation. I'm continuing the fight with a drug trial of Epcoritamab, a new medication not yet on the market, but showing great promise for resistant cancers like mine.

I'm the last member of the trio still singing the melody of non-Hodgkin's lymphoma. Will I be like Irv, promoted to the heavenly choir? Or will I be like Debbie, restored to health and using every ounce of energy for God, her family, and her ministry? Only God knows.

All I know is I hope to practice my theology. Either God is all-loving and all-powerful, or He is not. He is, and He is my Father, and I don't plan to live or die like an orphan!

Sometimes I've whimpered and whined. Then I remember whose child I am.

And I recall wise words from Oswald Chambers:

"Some moods don't go by praying; they go by kicking!"

Like Irv and Debbie, the other two members of our unexpected trio, I want the song of my life to echo the joyful theme, Soli Deo Gloria—Glory to God alone.

VALLEY OF TEARS
OCTOBER 2021

Her life was a song, and then—she was gone.
Amber was a daughter, a sister, an aunt, a friend, an author, a poet, a lover of creation, and a lover of God. She knew her worth; she was God's child, *Daughter of the Star Breather*. Amber even wrote a book by that title.

> "By the word of the LORD were the heavens made;
> and all the host of them by the breath of his
> mouth." –Psalm 33:6

Amber liked driving backcountry roads with the windows down, music loud, and wind blowing through her hair. She also delighted in the quiet, listening for the first spring peepers, and watching stars and fireflies. She loved the changes in the seasons.

I first met Amber at church when she was two years old, blonde hair hanging to her waist, and a wide, sweet smile. When it was prayer time the rest of us stayed in our pews, but not Amber. She slipped out into the aisle, knelt, and put her forehead on the floor. I grinned to see her little backside high in the air, but tears stung my eyes at the sweet reverence in one so young. From the first, she refused to leave church without hugging me. That hugging tradition continued until cancer and my oncologist's orders kept me from church. For almost twenty years, Amber blessed me with her hugs.

Long ago, I had a kids' club that met on Wednesday nights during adult prayer time. The kids got older and before I knew it, they were teens. School and sports' obligations claimed them one by one until only Amber was left on Wednesday nights. For years, the two of us met. We talked, laughed, cried, and prayed. Often, we leaned on the railing and watched the sun set over the fields west of the church. As she got older there were times when she would say something that made me wonder who the teacher was and who the learner. Near the end of Amber's life, we were two friends sharing what God was teaching us.

On the last night of her life, Amber went home, hugged her mom, and had cinnamon tea and cookies with her sister. Then the two of them stretched out on the trampoline laughing, talking, and watching the stars. It was late when Amber went back to another sister's house where she was living. She curled up in bed, and sometime in the early morning hours the Star Breather called her name. Amber went Home. Now she's looking at the stars from the other side. Amber wanted to know God better; now she does.

But she was only twenty-two.

The rest of us still journeying Home are walking through Baca, a weary weeping place, the valley of tears. We're happy for Amber but staggering with grief.

A pastor friend said, "Death is a defeated enemy, but make no mistake; it is still the enemy."

And a cruel enemy it is.

Our tears aren't without hope. Long ago, Amber knew she could never be good enough to get to heaven. That's an exercise in futility, right? It's like trying to jump across the Atlantic; you might jump farther than I, but neither of us is going to make it. Even as a child, Amber rejoiced with relief because she didn't have to be good enough to earn heaven. Jesus had lived the perfect life she couldn't and had died to take the punishment for her sin. She trusted Him as her Savior, and the minute she did, He entered her life and forgave her.

Amber and I sometimes talked about how it would have felt to have been Jesus, never to have known the awful feeling of guilt, and then to suddenly take into His heart every sin ever committed in the history of mankind and to feel the horrible guilt of it. It must have been every bit as excruciating as the physical pain of crucifixion, but He triumphed over sin, death, and hell. He made sin cease to exist for everyone who trusts Him as Savior. That's Amber's family, that's her friends, and that's me. We'll see her again. We'll spend eternity with her. I'll get more hugs. We'll watch together things even more beautiful than the sun setting west of our country church.

Until then, what do we do with all these tears?

The Psalmist said,

> "Blessed are those whose strength is in you, in whose heart are the highways to Zion. As they go through the Valley of Baca they make it a place of springs; the early rain also covers it with pools. They go from strength to strength; each one appears before God in Zion." –Psalm 84:5-7 ESV

Because of our tears we will someday provide refreshing

pools for others. Meanwhile, we go from strength to strength and lean on each other and on our God.

I picture our dear Lord Jesus holding a loaf of bread in His hands, blessing it, breaking it, and giving it to others. That's an allegory for life; we're blessed, broken, and given in a continuing cycle. I'm wondering where you are in that cycle. God bless you, wherever you are; don't lose hope!

Right now, all who love Amber are broken, standing in the valley of tears.

A friend from Ireland sang me a song today I'd never heard before. It had these words, "spreading a beautiful rainbow over the valley of tears." God is doing that for us.

George Matheson said,

"Show me that my tears have made my rainbow."

Our son, Dan, was thinking of Amber on his way to work this morning when he saw a rainbow in the western sky. He took a picture and sent it to me.

Dan's wife, Mindy, posted a lovely photo of fall leaves on Facebook with these words: "This morning on the way to school Ruby said, 'Momma, it's so peach outside. It's so pretty.' It was beautiful. The birds were singing, the rain was falling, and everything was some shade of Amber. I told her it was an Amber morning."

Yes, today was an Amber morning, and someday we'll have Amber mornings forever.

SUMMER SUN WAS ON HIS WINGS, WINTER IN HIS CRY
OCTOBER 2021

He knew.

How did knowing a winter more brutal than any other was coming for Him not darken His every thought, color His world with frigid foreboding, and freeze all thought of joy? And yet, somehow, it didn't.

Jesus was a paradox, a man of sorrows acquainted with grief[1] and yet more joyful than any other.[2]

Even though Jesus lived daily with the knowledge the cross was coming, He found Himself a magnet for small children who ran to Him, crowded around Him, and crawled onto His lap.

Kids aren't attracted to a man with a stern, frigid, grief-lined face.

Remember those lines in the movie, *Miracle on 34th Street*, when the lawyer pointed to the prosecutor and asked the little boy on the witness stand, "Could that man be Santa Claus?"

"No!"

"Why not?"

"Santa don't got no grumpy face!"

Though winter was in His cry—Jesus warned His disciples He was facing crucifixion—the summer sun was on His face. Children adored Him. I imagine they loved His laugh; I can't wait to someday hear that laugh myself!

I think of Jesus today when sickness, suffering, and death is wounding many people dear to my heart. I know where He found the sunshine on His wings despite everything. He found pure joy in communion with His Father.

He found it too in His love of nature. No wonder Jesus loved creation; He made everything and holds it together.[3]

In the loveliness of a created work, we see the beauty of the artist. When I admire a sunset, a flower, the patterns of clouds racing through a brilliant blue sky, I catch my breath at the thought of how beautiful the soul of Jesus must be.

Though winter was in His cry, Jesus noticed the beauty of wildflowers, the helplessness of lambs, and the needs of sparrows. He was the one who taught us, as George MacDonald said, that God sits beside each dying sparrow.

Picture Jesus walking those dusty backroads of Galilee, on His way to minister to yet another crowd of needy people, but taking time to talk to His Father, to notice the shepherd with his lambs, and to stoop and study the beauty of the lily. I imagine at night He smiled up at the stars He had named.

Jesus found joy even as His winter grew near.

Yes, my heart is heavy, and winter is in my cry for those I love who are suffering. But I relish the feeling of the sunshine on my face. I live in the minute and love the beauty of each tree vibrant with color, because winter is in their cry too.

In His creation, Jesus has given us more than beauty to enjoy; He has given us a glimpse of His radiant heart. When we appreciate beauty and thank Him for it, we find a bit of healing and peace.

Something Told the Wild Geese
by Rachel Field

"Something told the wild geese
It was time to go;
Though the fields lay golden
Something whispered, –'snow.'
Leaves were green and stirring,
Berries, luster-glossed,
But beneath warm feathers
Something cautioned, –'frost.'

All the sagging orchards
Steamed with amber spice,
But each wild breast stiffened
At remembered ice.

Something told the wild geese
It was time to fly–
Summer sun was on their wings,
Winter in their cry."

THE LITTLE CHURCH THAT COULD
OCTOBER 2021

It had been a glorious autumn day at the little church, the last day of October. The trees in the countryside were still wearing their best colors; their clothing had never looked more radiant. Still, as the sun began to lower in the west, the little church on the corner of two dirt roads sagged on its foundation and began to quietly weep. Tears streamed out of its windows and traced paths through the dust on its white sides.

A man with a long black coat flapping below his knees walked rapidly down the road. His walking stick barely touched the ground as little clouds of dirt stirred up around him but didn't seem to settle on him. His white hair touched his shoulders and made a startling contrast to the coat. He stopped suddenly, looked at the tears of the little church, and glanced up. Then he nodded, turned the corner, and sat on the church's cement steps.

"Do you mind if I rest here awhile, my friend?"

"All are welcome here," Little Church said, trying to keep from sobbing.

"I noticed your tears. What seems to be the problem?"

Little Church was used to solving problems for others, not telling others its difficulties. It studied the man sitting on its steps. He had kind, blue eyes above a neat, white beard. Little Church was sure he'd never met him before. Did he dare share his burdens with this stranger?

"Are you from around here?"

"No, my friend, I'm just passing through. I hold many secrets in my heart. Yours are safe with me."

At that, Little Church stopped trying to hold back its sobs. Out spilled its whole bitter story of better days, of days when little children filled pews, of days when there was barely enough room to hold all the people.

"Those were my better days. But there were so many things I couldn't do that other, bigger churches could. I couldn't have a variety of Sunday school classes. I couldn't have wonderful programs and activities for each age group; I didn't have the space or enough help. I couldn't keep up with what the people wanted, and I've lost so many of them. They left for bigger and better. I've failed the Master, and I'm worried about tomorrow. We have so few children now; who will keep me going so I can be a light here on the corner until Jesus comes?"

"Why do you say the former days were better than these? Can you judge like our Master can judge? And as for tomorrow, like my friend Elisabeth Elliot once said, 'Tomorrow belongs to God. Tomorrow is none of your business!'"

"Do you know Elisabeth Elliot?"

"Oh yes. We talk often."

"But. . . Elisabeth Elliot is dead!"

"And you're a white frame building, but we're talking, so there's that. But remember, tomorrow is none of your business!"

The words were stern, but the merry laughter and the kind tone soothed the heart of the little church. Where had this wise man with white hair and long black coat come from?

"You don't know which of your days will count most for eternity," the man continued. "God isn't finished with you yet. So, perhaps you should focus on what you can do in the future instead of what you can't."

All was quiet for several moments. A soft breeze blew from the west where the sun was becoming a glowing, red orb. The very air around the little church seemed to hint of heaven.

The man spoke again, "When Jesus lived on earth, He walked dirt roads much like these. He didn't have any big programs to entertain people. He had no involved children's clubs that required many workers; He just took the children on His lap and blessed them. Jesus was a servant Who taught with love. Can you listen each Sunday for the 'whisper of His sandaled feet' and follow Him? Can you teach, love, and serve?"

"I can. I can listen for Him. 'Teach. Love. And Serve.' That's always been my song, but fear stole my words. Thank you for singing them back to me."

"You're welcome," the man said. "I best be on my way before darkness falls."

He stood, stretched, and picked up his walking stick. Then he headed west down the dusty road into the sunset.

"Wait!" Little Church called. "I want to remember the man who put the song back into my heart. What's your name?"

In a voice that echoed like thunder, the man said, "You may call me Gabriel."

The black coat turned brighter than the sun, and in a flash of lightning, he disappeared.

Little Church once again stood tall on its foundation and never again forgot what it *could* do. For some, it would not be enough, but Little Church would teach, love, and serve with joy. And it would remember that tomorrow was none of its business.

A GRATEFUL HEART
NOVEMBER 2021

"Emma," Mia whispered, "you still awake?"

"Yep. Just looking for a happy from today to think about before I fall asleep."

"You do that every night. Well, you can stop trying to find your happy. I've got one for you. Mom and Dad are taking us to Alabama for Thanksgiving! We're staying in an ocean front condo. But don't tell Mom I told you. Maybe she wants to surprise you."

"I've always wanted to see the ocean! What's it like?"

"You know how much you love Lake Michigan? It's like that only way better. And we'll walk the beach and collect shells. We're going to have so much fun!"

"Mia, you're the best foster sister I've ever had!"

Mia laughed. "I think I'm the only foster sister you've ever had. Didn't you say there were only boys in all those other foster homes?"

Emma shuddered at the memory of what had happened in some of those homes, things she'd never tell Mia. In her thirteen years, she'd been in eight different homes, and this was the first place she'd felt safe. But she wasn't going to think about those other places now, not when she could imagine sinking her toes into white sand in Alabama!

Emma usually woke earlier than Mia and helped Nancy in the kitchen before everyone left for work or school. She'd long ago learned things went better for her in the foster homes if she made herself useful.

As she hurried to the kitchen, Emma wondered if Nancy would tell her about the trip. Thanksgiving was only a few days away.

"Sit down, Emma." Nancy sighed.

Have I done something wrong? I can't think of anything, but she looks so upset!

"Mia doesn't know this yet. Her dad's company has transferred him to Alabama. We're going down there for Thanksgiving, and we'll be looking for a home to buy. It's going to be hard for Mia to leave her school, her friends, and you. We can't take you out of state, Emma. I want to make this as easy as possible for Mia. I'm trusting you not to say anything to her; we'll tell her when we're in Alabama. You'll go to the sitter's when we leave for our trip. By the time we return, you'll be in another foster home. I think it's better for Mia this way. It's going to break her heart, and that's partly my fault. I've let her get too close to you. I thought she understood you were only a foster child, but I've heard her refer to you as 'my sister' several times lately. Can I trust you not to say anything to her?"

Emma nodded mutely, tears running down her face.

Am I just a piece of furniture to get shoved aside or donated to someone else? Don't you care about me at all?

Nancy raised surprised eyebrows. "Don't take this so hard, Emma. You've been in more foster homes than I can count. Surely you didn't expect us to adopt you?"

It was only when she heard the words, Emma realized that was exactly what she'd hoped. Mia was like a sister to her; she'd hoped perhaps Mia's parents would learn to love her too.

Now I'm going to be alone again.

Emma remembered words she'd memorized as a little girl when someone had taken her to church, words Jesus had said: *"I will never leave you or forsake you."*

It felt like God Himself was standing next to her, lifting her chin, putting steel into her spine.

Emma heard Mia coming downstairs. Nancy gave her a sharp, warning look.

Mia hugged Emma. "Good morning, sister!"

Emma's heart twisted.

"You girls need to pack right after breakfast," Nancy said. "Mia, you're packing for Alabama, and Emma's going to pack to stay with the sitter."

"What! Emma isn't coming with us? Then I don't want to go."

"Mia," her mom said, "we need to spend some time as a family. Emma understands. We've talked."

Mia was furious and crying. "Emma *is* family. She's as much family as you and Dad."

Nancy's lips tightened into a thin line. "This is exactly why we need to spend time as just a family."

Mia knew when she'd lost a battle. She sighed.

"Emma, I'll bring you back lots of shells, okay?"

A few hours later, two thirteen-year-old girls parted in the driveway, one to go on vacation, the other to go back into an overwhelmed foster system. Mia thought they were going to be apart for only a few days. Emma knew it would be for years, or maybe forever.

"Mia, I want you to remember something Abraham Lincoln said."

Mia smiled through tears. "You can't go on vacation with me, and you want to talk about Abraham Lincoln? Sometimes you're too funny, Emma. Okay. What did he say?"

"He said, 'Most people are about as happy as they make up their minds to be.'"

"So that's why you try to think of a happy every night before you go to sleep? You've made up your mind to be happy?"

"Enough goodbyes!" Nancy said. "We need to get going, and the sitter is here for Emma."

Emma watched Mia and her parents get into the taxi. The last leaf fell from the maple and danced its way down to the driveway. Emma imagined herself the tree, lifting bare arms in mute appeal to heaven.

The sitter tossed Emma's belongings into the car and backed out of the driveway.

"Will I be at your house for Thanksgiving?" Emma was surprised at how timid her voice sounded.

"Sorry, Emma. Your case worker is picking you up tomorrow. I don't know where you'll be for Thanksgiving. I hope you'll get a good turkey dinner wherever it is."

Emma stared out of the window at the bleak November landscape. She thought for a minute about warm, white sandy beaches, Alabama sunshine, and collecting shells with Mia. She let herself feel how wonderful it would have been to be Mia's sister. Those dreams were gone, and who knew what else life might take from her. Well, no one was going to get her grateful heart. That belonged only to her and God. She was barely more than a child, but somehow, she knew her survival depended on keeping it.

"Open your hand," the sitter said softly. She placed a tiny, beautiful shell into Emma's outstretched palm. "I went to

Alabama once and brought back a few shells. I want you to have this one."

Emma whispered her thanks and stared at the shell; its pale pink center swirled into smooth pearl, fragile as a dream, beautiful as hope. Her hand closed around it.

WINTER OF MY CONTENT
DECEMBER 2021

There I was, enjoying the Fourth of July parade, when a freak snowstorm came from nowhere. Sometimes it rains on the parade, but snow? The first few flakes quickly turned into a whiteout. As winds howled and the temperature dropped sixty degrees in six minutes, bystanders rushed for cars. The parade halted, and participants hurried to find the closest shelter.

Okay, so that didn't exactly happen, but it's true metaphorically speaking. There I was, enjoying the long, lingering summer of my life. Winter was far away, or so I thought, and the blizzard caught me unprepared, still wearing my summer flip-flops.

Are we ever ready to get old? Isn't old always at least twenty years older than we are? That's how I used to think.

I'm still shocked at the little old gray-haired lady who stares back at me from the mirror, and then we both start singing, "It's the little old lady from Pasadena, go Granny, go Granny, go Granny, go!" And we laugh.

This is, I think, only the beginning of my winter; it could be the end. I don't know. No one really knows how long a winter may last. When I was young, I planned this winter in my imagination. I'd be a briskly walking, still jump roping, up for any adventure grandma. When I wasn't having adventures with my grandchildren, I'd sit by a fire and read and write. I'd enjoy the short but sweet winter twilights and then smile myself to sleep with happy memories of yesterday and robust plans for tomorrow.

I didn't imagine cancer, or what it would do to dreams of the kind of old lady I'd be. I still have adventures. It's an adventure to get from the bed to the car in one piece! It's an adventure to fit all the tests and doctors visits into the calendar. Sometimes, when I'm feeling extra daring, I even take a shower. . . and skip the nap after!

This is not, however, the winter of my discontent. I'm not unhappy. I find happiness in different ways than I'd imagined. Today I woke from a nap to hear feet on the stairs. I don't know which of the three people who live with me was going upstairs, but I smiled. It made me feel warm and happy to hear footsteps on the stairs and know they belonged to someone dear to me. Had I been the jump roping, busy grandma I'd imagined, I don't think I'd have ever known how sweet it is to hear footsteps of a loved one on the stairs.

Small blessings bring grace to my heart and instant tears to my eyes. Today my sister told me my brother-in-law, who's alone in a hospital in New York City and very sick, was out of an expensive skin cream he really needs. The hospital doctor, without being asked, went to a drugstore, used his own money, and bought the cream.

When my brother-in-law tried to pay him, the doctor said, "Nope. We're good."

I've been thinking about that often today, the kindness of

strangers, and how much more it means to someone who is sick and hurting.

God has many earth angels, and as someone once said, "Human kindness is Jesus showing His hands."

I'm grateful for human kindness and hundreds of other small things I never thought much about before: smiles, waves, hugs around the knees from a tiny granddaughter, a text from one of my adult kids or in-law kids, the changing slant of light with the seasons, and the quiet, country view from my bedroom window.

Yes, I'm sick. Yes, I've lost people dear to me. Yes, this is hard. But when I lie in my cozy bed, even when my sore bones don't exactly let me get comfortable, the music starts. Under the ice of my storms, a spring stream flows, and it sings to me. It sings of grace and mercy. It hums of love and laughter. Sometimes lyrics run through my mind, as eclectic as I am: old hymns, Ron Hamilton, southern gospel, old time country, music from high school.

Occasionally I sing along, "You're a mean one, Mr. Grinch."

With each new medical test, I'm like the Grinch's cartoon sleigh tipping back and forth on that impossible precipice of a mountain.

Which way will I slide? And yet, I'm at peace. I'm wrapped in a cozy blanket made of the kindness of family, friends, and strangers. The music grows faint sometimes, but it's there when I get quiet enough to listen. The winter winds howl, and everything freezes, but the spring stream flows under the ice, and I'm content.

These days, the stream under the ice is lit with tiny white lights and sings Christmas songs to me.

The winter of Jesus's life came when He was so young. The shadow of a cross fell over the manger; His birth was the prelude to His death. Yet what joy He found along the way, even though the road led to Calvary.

> "Those who watched Jesus dying saw nothing but loss and tragedy. Yet at the heart of that darkness the divine mercy was powerfully at work, bringing about pardon and forgiveness for us. God's salvation came into the world through suffering, so his saving grace and power can work in our lives more and more as we go through difficulty and sorrow. There's mercy deep inside our storms."
> –Timothy Keller

Oh, that's for sure. "There's mercy deep inside our storms." And that's why this is the winter of my content. God's at work, and all is well.

OUR PRACTICALLY PERFECT CHRISTMAS
DECEMBER 2021

Magic gently falls over our home like a blanket of snow each family Christmas. I can't explain it, but even with thirteen grandchildren, no one ever gets sick. The twenty-three of us manage to gather every year without having to reschedule the date. The cousins play like the angels they are, and for only that one day, siblings don't get frustrated with each other for invading personal space.

And the adults? The eleven of us, who usually have twenty different opinions on almost everything, merge into a spirit of love and unity beautiful to behold. If people disagree, they smile and let it go. Not only do we love each other; we like each other. We like everything about each other because we're family. After all, it's Christmas.

Christmas carols play softly on someone's phone, and the children wait quietly as each opens a gift in turn. It's never too noisy. You'd hardly know thirteen children were here.

And then, we feast on the roast beast. Just for that one day, nothing burns or undercooks.

As we gather at tables with only peace and love in our

hearts, it's not unusual for someone to say, "Look, Grandma! It started snowing!"

And if you believe that piece of fiction, congratulations, you won a GOTYA—gullible of the year award.

Let's get real here. Getting the twenty-three of us together is a gymnastic feat and can't be accomplished some years despite amazing contortions. Kids get sick, and we try to reschedule, but sometimes we end up with two celebrations instead of one.

Kids wake up sick on family Christmas morning. Siblings remove each other from their personal spaces. And we eleven adults? I know how to read faces. I've known these people a long time. I see the raised eyebrow; I can tell when someone is biting a tongue. And the kids' noise? I love it, but I think next year I'll put ear plugs in everyone's Christmas stockings to prevent hearing loss.

One Christmas, a little grandson started not feeling well and lay on the couch most of the time. He went home and threw up. Poor kid! We shouldn't have laughed when we heard about what he said after getting sick, but we did.

"It's still corn! How can it still be corn when I ate it!"

There was one Christmas John and I had to leave because a church member needed us.

There were two Christmases when a grandchild fell into the Christmas tree—the same grandchild. It's one of my favorite memories.

The same grandchild, when a bit older, told me at Christmas, "You're getting really old, Grandma. I guess pretty soon you'll be dead."

I adore him; he makes me laugh!

There was a not at all funny Christmas when parents had to rush a very sick child to the emergency room. And one when our fireman son had to leave. And one where a whole family of littles got sick because of germs caught at Grandma and Grandpa's house.

I could continue, but you get the idea.

I blame Mom and Dad Poole for starting the tradition of holiday trouble. Once Mom put dinner roles in the oven in a paper bag to warm them. The bag caught on fire, and she yelled for Dad. He came running in his underwear, grabbed the rolls, ran out to the back porch, and threw the burning mess into the yard. We all laughed for years about Dad running outside in his underwear and wondered how many of their neighbors laughed too. And my husband remembers the year of the famous seafood dip that gave everyone in his family food poisoning.

We have enjoyed a few practically perfect Christmases when everything was like a storybook. But no matter what happens, every Christmas is perfect for me, and here's why.

As imperfect as the twenty-three of us are, we all really do love each other, and I love each one of them fiercely. I hold them in my thoughts, heart, and prayers always. I would do anything for them, and when we're all together, no matter what happens, I catch my breath at the perfectly imperfect beauty of it all. Just having everyone together is magical for me.

And then the best part happens. Before we open gifts, a grandchild reads to us verses from Luke chapter two. Megan, our oldest granddaughter, read for many years. I think she was only four or five when she started. When she got older, we passed the honor down to her younger brother, Reece. When he began, he was so young he mispronounced some words, and anyone who snickered got a grandma scowl from me. Reece is still our reader.

John hands him the Bible, and Reece begins to read,

¹And it came to pass in those days, that there went out a decree from Caesar Augustus that all the world should be taxed.

² (And this taxing was first made when Cyrenius was governor of Syria.)

³ And all went to be taxed, every one into his own city.

⁴ And Joseph also went up from Galilee, out of the city of Nazareth, into Judaea, unto the city of David, which is called Bethlehem; (because he was of the house and lineage of David:)

⁵ To be taxed with Mary his espoused wife, being great with child.

⁶ And so it was, that, while they were there, the days were accomplished that she should be delivered.

⁷ And she brought forth her firstborn son, and wrapped him in swaddling clothes, and laid him in a manger; because there was no room for them in the inn.

⁸ And there were in the same country shepherds abiding in the field, keeping watch over their flock by night.

⁹ And, lo, the angel of the Lord came upon them, and the glory of the Lord shone round about them: and they were sore afraid.

¹⁰ And the angel said unto them, Fear not: for, behold, I bring you good tidings of great joy, which shall be to all people.

¹¹ For unto you is born this day in the city of David a Saviour, which is Christ the Lord.

¹² And this shall be a sign unto you; Ye shall find the babe wrapped in swaddling clothes, lying in a manger.

¹³ And suddenly there was with the angel a multitude of the heavenly host praising God, and saying,

14 Glory to God in the highest, and on earth peace, good will toward men.

15 And it came to pass, as the angels were gone away from them into heaven, the shepherds said one to another, Let us now go even unto Bethlehem, and see this thing which is come to pass, which the Lord hath made known unto us.

16 And they came with haste, and found Mary, and Joseph, and the babe lying in a manger.

17 And when they had seen it, they made known abroad the saying which was told them concerning this child.

18 And all they that heard it wondered at those things which were told them by the shepherds.

19 But Mary kept all these things, and pondered them in her heart.

20 And the shepherds returned, glorifying and praising God for all the things that they had heard and seen, as it was told unto them.

Yes, they are good tidings of great joy. When I hear my beloved grandson read those old familiar verses, the joy fills my heart and runs out of my eyes and down my cheeks. It's Christmas. It's not just practically perfect; it's perfect in every way!

Come to think of it, the only perfect thing about the first Christmas was the baby born in the manger, born to die for our sins.

I leave you with a Merry Christmas from my heart, dear friends, and a thank you for traveling the backroads with me this year. Enjoy your imperfect Christmas! And now, please excuse me. The ham is drying out; the sweet potato casserole caught fire, and someone, you know who, fell into the Christmas tree.

MY BEST GIFT
DECEMBER 2021

Growing up, we Piarulli kids never thought of ourselves as poor. We were like many other large families of the 1950s and 1960s when one paycheck had to stretch too far. It never occurred to us to wonder if other kids were still hungry when supper was finished; that was just how life was. It's only in looking back and remembering snatches of conversations that I realize how hard my parents struggled financially. And yet, we were better off than many.

Somehow, Mom and Dad managed to give us kids a wonderful Christmas every year. Perhaps my memory is tangled with stars and silver bells, but I recall most Christmas days as white with snow. Each strand of tinsel hung perfectly straight on our tree strung with lights, and the house smelled wonderfully of pine.

Carefully wrapped gifts, not many but more than enough, were piled under the tree, and for a few days of the year, everything was close to perfect.

Until the arrival of *that hideous thing*.

We came home from school one day laughing, cheeks glowing, and stomping snow off our boots.

What was that?

We stared.

Mom stood next to it, smiling proudly, waiting for our reaction. *That hideous thing* was a tree about three feet tall with skimpy, silver-colored branches. At its foot was a color wheel.

"Wait until you see this!"

Mom plugged in the color wheel, and it rotated, turning the branches red, blue, green, and yellow. All ugly. All artificial. All hideous.

I wish we'd been more considerate of Mom's feelings; she obviously thought she'd found a lovely treasure, but we hated it. And we said so. We disliked it more every year. There were no more real trees, no rooms filled with the scent of pine. The tree stood on an end table, not on the floor where a proper, real Christmas tree should stand.

True, as Mom pointed out, it didn't drop needles or make a mess. We wished it would drop its needles, but it endured with the tenacity of Methuselah. It's probably still alive in a landfill somewhere!

But Christmas gifts were wonderful when I was a child. When we were very young, Mom always put two unwrapped dolls on the couch for Mary and me. The first one to the sofa got first pick of a doll. Aunt Mary, who owned a dress factory, gave each of us girls a beautiful thick sweater every year. One year, Grandma gave Mary and me teddy bears we cherished.

When we went to bed at night, one of us would ask, "Does your teddy bear love my teddy bear?"

"My teddy bear loves your teddy bear if your teddy bear loves my teddy bear."

Once it was settled that the bears and their owners loved each other, we slept, each holding her bear close. I don't know what happened to my bear, but Mary had hers until recently. Those bears were among our favorite gifts.

When I got a little older, I looked under the tree for a book shaped package and was never disappointed. My new Nancy Drew book was there, and I devoured it before Christmas Day ended. I loved those books.

One year, Dad told us to come outside to see our gift, a lovely wooden toboggan. That was an amazing present!

My favorite gift didn't come from Mom and Dad, Aunt Mary, Grandma, or any family member. It didn't even come at Christmas. It came from someone who terrified me, Mrs. Green.

Mrs. Green was a fearful presence who ruled children's church. I'm sure she must have been a nice person, but I couldn't see it back then. Her stern persona and hawklike eyes made me shudder.

One Sunday, Mrs. Green used a flannel covered board with flannel illustrations that stuck to it. We called them flannelgraph figures. She put up pictures of heaven and talked about how wonderful it would be. Next, she did something I don't recommend for small children; she placed fiery pictures of hell.

"Boys and girls, don't think that because Jesus, God's Son, came to earth as a baby, grew up, and died on the cross to pay for the sins of the world that you're going to heaven. It doesn't work that way. Don't think that because your mom and dad bring you to church every Sunday, you're going to heaven; it doesn't work that way!"

She jabbed a bony finger at the flames.

What was she saying? I wasn't going to heaven just because Jesus died for me, and I came to church every Sunday?

She had my attention. How was I going to get into heaven? Whatever it took, I'd do it!

Up went a picture of a cross, and the explanation that Jesus died for our sins. For my sin. Something stirred deeply in my young heart.

What kind of love was this that someone would die for me?

Mrs. Green put flannelgraph gifts on the board.

"Jesus died to give you salvation from sin and a home in heaven. But does looking at a gift make it yours? No. You have to reach out and take it."

So how did I take this gift? I had to admit to God I was a sinner. Well, God and I both knew that! I needed to tell Him I believed Jesus died for me and ask Him to save me. Mrs. Green told us to bow our heads for silent prayer.

"If any of you took that gift and accepted Jesus as your Savior, raise your hand. I'd like to talk to you."

What? Talk to Mrs. Green all by myself?

I didn't raise my hand. My heart was full of faith and joy, but I saw no compelling reason to become a martyr for my faith on the first day I had it. Alone with Mrs. Green? That was worse than Daniel being thrown into the lion's den!

I never did thank Mrs. Green for giving me the best gift of all. When I get to heaven, I'll look her up and do it. Maybe. If she doesn't still terrify me.

I read somewhere Patrick Henry said the gift he wished he could give everyone was his faith in Jesus Christ. I wish I could give that to you too, but you'll have to accept the gift yourself. I hope you will.

Jesus grows sweeter to me every year, and He fills my heart with hope and joy that run clear and deep under the ice of life's many storms.

I'm still pondering the question my child's heart asked so many years ago: *What kind of love is this that someone would die for me?*

It's not just grace; it's amazing grace, a grace that came to earth as a tiny baby who gave us a way Home to God

Merry Christmas, dear friends! See you at Home.

P.S. Mary, my teddy bear still loves your teddy bear, always.

THE TRUE MIRACLE
DECEMBER 2021

Agatha raised herself on her elbow and gagged weakly into the bowl at her side. She heard the curtain to her room slide back.

"Please, go away," she whispered.

Mary and Dorcas heard her, but they did not go away. Dorcas dipped a cloth into cool water and held it to her forehead as Mary gently supported her shoulders until the rest of her breakfast left her body.

Tears ran down Agatha's cheeks. She'd always been a strong, proud woman, and she didn't want her friends to see her like this.

"Go, now, please," she said.

Instead of leaving, they sat on the floor next to her mat.

"Jesus is back here in Capernaum," Mary said with quiet excitement.

Dorcas nodded. "He can tell you what's wrong with you, and He can heal you. You know He can."

"Let us help you get to Jesus," Mary begged. "You can lean on us."

Agatha shook her head wearily.

"Just let me die in peace. I know what's wrong with me. I've told you before. My father taught me that three-thousand years ago ancient Egyptians cauterized breast tumors with a tool they called the fire drill. Four-hundred years ago a Greek physician, Hippocrates, called tumors carcinos and carcinoma. And in the last few decades the Roman physician, Celsus, translated the Greek word into the Roman word 'cancer.' I have cancer. It's all through my body. Look at me! No one can help me now, not even Yahweh!"

She closed her eyes and threw one thin arm over them.

Agatha's friends did look at her and then at each other with tears in their eyes. In the last year, she'd lost a third of her body weight. Her soft snores let them know she was asleep.

"Mary," Dorcas said, "sometimes I think her Greek father educated her too much for her own good. She has too much learning to have any room for faith."

Dorcas shook her head. "I don't think it's that. I think she's too tired to have faith, so we're going to have to have it for her. If she can't remember the song of her heart, we can, and we'll sing it back to her."

"You speak in riddles. What do you have in mind?"

"Come," Dorcas whispered, and the two friends tiptoed out of the house.

As they walked down the dusty street, they made their plans.

"It might work," Mary agreed excitedly. "We'd only need four good sized boys. She weighs barely more than a child."

∽

AGATHA CRIED out in terror and woke from her dream.

Let me die in peace I said to my friends, but there is no

peace. My sins are like tormenting spirits haunting me waking and sleeping!

"Why did you name me Agatha, Father?" she whispered to his memory. "It means good woman, but I am not one. I have no sins of the flesh to confess, but oh these secret sins of the spirit eat at me more than the cancer. The envy, the spite, the selfishness in my heart! If only I could leave my sin behind when I die, I'd gladly die this minute to be free of it! But will it follow me into the great unknown? You taught me so much, Father. Why didn't you teach me this? I've followed all of Mother's Jewish customs, but were they enough? None of the sacrifices have set me free from myself."

Agatha turned on her side and sobbed herself back to sleep. She was only semi-conscious when she felt her mat being lifted from the floor. Through tear-swollen eyes, she squinted up at four smiling lads.

"Where are you taking me?" she cried in alarm.

"It's alright," Mary said, reaching for her hand.

Dorcas took her other hand. "We're taking you to Jesus."

"No!" She struggled to sit, but she was too weak. "He cannot help me. Please don't carry me into the streets like this where people will see me."

Her friends pulled soft coverings up to her chin and pleaded with their eyes. How could she refuse such love?

Through the streets of Capernaum they went until they came to the house where Jesus was teaching. It was one of the larger homes, able to hold about fifty people crowded closely together, but the crowd had spilled out of the door and stood deep around the windows, a quiet crowd, straining to hear every word of the Master.

"We cannot get through," one of the lads said. "Shall we go back?"

"No!" Dorcas nodded at the outside staircase. "Carry her to the roof."

The boys looked apprehensive but obeyed. Even Mary was alarmed.

"Dorcas, what do you have in mind?"

"Do you believe Jesus can heal her?"

"You know I absolutely do!"

"Then get ready to get dirty!"

Dorcas had to promise the boys they wouldn't get into trouble with their parents, and she would pay for damages before they agreed to help, but soon six pairs of hands were digging through the mud roof. Mud and debris began falling into peoples' hair, and the crowd looked up in amazement and anger. Jesus laughed.

As soon as the hole was big enough, two of the boys jumped down, while Mary, Dorcas, and the other two lowered Agatha on her mat. There she lay, in front of Jesus. He looked deep into her eyes.

"Welcome, Agatha, good woman.'"

She shook her head, tears running unhindered down her face. Agatha was in the presence of pure goodness and had never felt her sinfulness more. She groaned, and it wasn't from the pain of the cancer. She looked away from Jesus. How could sin look at such holiness?

Jesus took her two thin hands in his two strong ones.

"Look at me, my daughter," He said in a voice of love. "Your sins are forgiven."

Agatha could almost see them leave, those heavy condemning spirits, the ghostly chains of sins past, present, and future. She felt so light and free, so full of joy!

Agatha looked up through the hole in the roof at her friends. They were frowning. This is not why they'd brought her to Jesus. They were quite unhappy with this outcome.

Couldn't they understand? She didn't care about the cancer in her body anymore. Everyone died sometime. The cancer in her spirit was gone, and that was the true miracle! She really was a good woman now with a goodness not her own.

She could hear others in the crowd murmuring, some wearing the robes of the elite Pharisees.

"Who does this Jesus think he is? Only God can forgive sins."

Jesus nodded at Agatha.

"Get ready," He whispered. Then with a commanding shout He ordered, "So they will know the Son of Man has power of earth to forgive sins, Agatha, good woman, take up your bed, and walk!"

Jesus stretched His hand down and lifted her up. She felt the cancer leaving her body and the strength of youth flowing into her.

"How?" she whispered. "How?"

Now Jesus looked sad. "You'll know later when you stand at the foot of my cross. Go now. Live your life in joy."

She'd never known, with all her learning, that holiness was just another word for happiness.

Agatha rolled up her mat and looked up at the roof. How was she going to get back up through that hole?

"You might try going out the door," Jesus said. And again He laughed.

She laughed too, and then the whole room was laughing. The crowd parted, making a way for her to get through. People patted her back.

"Go with Yahweh, good woman!" someone shouted.

That was exactly what she intended to do.

"Happiness is a long walk with a friend." –Unknown

"In life, it's not where you go, it's who you travel with." – Charles Schulz

A Few More Ramblings

1
LET'S GET RICH

You never thought you'd get paid for doing something you love, like taking a walk.

Your sweatshirt is cozy warm against the brisk breeze as you walk down a country backroad. Colorful leaves dance their way from branches over your head to join the piles on the ground. You feel like a kid again, so you kick the leaves for the fun of it, and an envelope tumbles out. Inside, you find ten crisp, new one-hundred-dollar bills. You've read about these new bills, but you haven't seen them yet.

Are these real?

You run your finger along Ben Franklin's shoulder, and it feels bumpy; it's supposed to on the new bills. There's so much gold: a gold liberty bell, a gold inkwell, and a gold feather pen. The 3D security ribbon changes from $100 to bells as you move a bill from side to side. A bell in the copper inkwell turns green as you shift the bill, and the large 100 numeral turns from copper to green when you tilt it. You hold the bill to the sun and see a faint portrait of Ben Franklin in the watermark.

These are real alright. Who ditches a grand in leaves on the side of a dirt road?

No one, that's who; someone must be desperate to find this money.

You notify the police and advertise you've found a certain sum in a remote area. You get a few phone calls, but no one can tell you the amount or the location, so you call the police back. They tell you to keep the money.

That's one walk that paid off.

I read about someone who got paid for doing something I love, reading. It happened way back in 1891.

Vido Mati, a Spanish student, was researching for a school project. He hauled a dusty old philosophy book off a high shelf. It looked like it hadn't been read much since it had been published. Vido opened the book, and a thin piece of paper fell out.

The paper was dated June 2, 1741. It was the author's will, leaving all his money to the first person to open his book after he died. One-hundred-and fifty years later, Vido was that person. He became fifty-thousand pounds richer because he decided to read an old book.

I found money in a book once. An envelope with a note enclosed fell out of a library book.

The note read, "Will you please renew my book? Enclosed please find my fifteen cents fine."

I gave the money to the librarian. My bank account hasn't grown because of my love of books, but reading has made me rich.

When I was a child, we moved often, and it wasn't easy to say goodbye to familiar places or good friends. The friends in my book world stayed the same. I could always visit the *Little Women* or one of The Five Little Peppers.

As I got older, I loved all the Nancy Drew, Cherry Ames,

and Donna Parker books. I didn't so much read books as I lived in them.

I was still quite young, perhaps in junior high, when I read *Stepping Heavenward* by Elizabeth Prentiss. That book, written in 1869, spoke to my heart as though the author was sitting next to me. It was, perhaps, the first book that showed me the power words have to speak through the centuries. That little book opened my eyes to a deeper walk with God and made me richer spiritually.

John D. Snider said,

> "Books are a treasure chest which yields greater riches the more it is rifled."

François Fénelon, a great reader and author, wrote,

> "If the riches of the Indies or the wealth of all the crowned heads of Europe were given to me in exchange for my love of reading, I would spurn them all."

If you are a book lover like I am, we're in good company. William Gladstone, the famous British statesmen, lived to be eighty-eight, and until the day he died, he carried a book in his pocket so he could spend any spare minute reading.

One of my favorite writers, F.W. Boreham, promised himself he'd buy and read a book a week, and he kept that vow for more than twenty years.

A great preacher, Charles Spurgeon, read six books a week in addition to sometimes preaching eight to ten times a week.

Thomas Edison often stayed up reading until two o'clock in the morning, despite needing to be up and dressed by seven. And he was eighty years old when he did this.

Books enrich my circle of friends now the same way they did when I was the little girl who moved often. Some of my best friends live on dusty shelves between two hard covers, and I'm not alone in feeling that way.

Charlotte Brontë said of her books,

> "What, I sometimes ask, would I do without them? I have recourse to them as to friends."

Oswald Chambers agreed:

> "I do thank God for my books with every fibre of my being. Friends that are ever true and ever your own."

Books greatly enrich our thoughts. Thomas S. Kepler wrote about books,

> "These are a stimulating fellowship; had I not met them I wonder what my own thoughts might be."

Books can also open our hearts to goodness.

> "We sometimes take a partiality to books, as to characters, not on account of any brilliant intellect or striking peculiarity they boast, but for the sake of something good, delicate, and genuine." –Charlotte Brontë

So, let's walk together in our imaginations down some back-country road. As we walk, maybe we can talk about something Annie Dillard said,

"There are people who, if you told them the world would end in ten minutes, would try to decide—quickly—what to read."

As we walk and talk about books, let's remember to look up at the sunshine, feel the wind on our faces, and kick a pile of leaves every now and then. Nature tells her stories too, to anyone young at heart enough to listen.

When we get to the fork in the road and say goodbye, we'll be richer because of the time we've spent together, and the books we carry in our hearts.

2
THEY CALLED HER GRANDMA G.

On a good Sunday, the white frame church on the corner of two dirt roads had forty people in its pews. It was a good Sunday; there were forty-five there, and they had to set up extra chairs in the back. That sometimes happened on potluck Sundays. The congregation was famous for its country cooking. Everyone stayed after the morning service for the potluck, everyone except Grandpa and Grandma G. Grandpa G. hated potlucks. No one knew why.

He and Grandma G. were the church's oldest members. They'd attended long before half the congregation had been born. Grandpa and Grandma G. weren't related to anyone in the church, not anymore, but in that church, everyone was family. Whenever anyone under the age of eighteen had a birthday, they got a card in the mail with a stick of gum enclosed. It was signed, "Love, Grandma G." One little girl who got many lovely gifts for her seventh birthday said that piece of gum was her favorite.

Grandma G. had grown up in the country church, and her family had been none too sure about the soldier who'd visited and fallen in love with their beautiful girl, but their worry had proved unfounded, as many worries do.

Grandpa G., at the wish of her parents, had joined the church the day he'd married Grandma G., when he was nineteen, and she was seventeen. The two of them had celebrated seventy anniversaries sitting in the same pew, left side, third from the front.

That pew was empty this potluck Sunday. Even a stranger would have felt the subdued atmosphere. It was as tangible as the old, frayed green hymnals in the pew racks. The huge bouquets of fading flowers and tears on faces testified there had been a recent funeral at the church. Grandpa G. had died.

Usually, the congregation's singing echoed off the old rafters, but today was different. Even the elderly pastor couldn't muster up his usual volume. He kept looking down at the flowers on the communion table.

Why didn't I throw those out? They look terrible. And I should have picked a different hymn. Half the people are crying instead of singing.

The pastor persevered, though; if he'd been the type to give up easily, he never would have stayed in a tiny church for fifty years, loving on the broken and the hurting.

So, he kept the melody going the best he could: "Will the circle, be unbroken?"

Suddenly the old, wooden doors in the back opened, and the unmistakable tap of a cane sounded on the wooden floor. No one pounded a cane like Grandma G.

No one had expected Grandma G. to come, not so soon after the death of her beloved husband.

But up the aisle she came, adding her strong, if shaky, alto voice to the preacher's melody: "By and by, yes, by and by? In a better home awaiting in the sky, in the sky?"

Up the middle aisle she came until she got to her pew, left

side, third from the front. Cane tapping, tapping, she walked all the way to the left end of the pew until she was next to the window where she could look out and see the corn growing.

Not realizing the pastor was on the third verse, Grandma G. started singing the first, and the pastor and congregation joined in with her. The volume picked up, and Grandma G. sang loudest of all:

> "There are loved ones in the glory,
>> Whose dear forms you often miss;
>> When you close your earthly story,
>> Will you join them in their bliss?
>
> Will the circle be unbroken
>> By and by, by and by?
>> In a better home awaiting
>> In the sky, in the sky.
>> In the joyous days of childhood,
>> Oft they told of wondrous love,
>> Pointed to the dying Savior;
>> Now they dwell with Him above.
>> You remember songs of heaven
>> Which you sang with childish voice,
>> Do you love the hymns they taught you,
>> Or are songs of earth your choice?
>> You can picture happy gath'rings
>> 'Round the fireside long ago,
>> And you think of tearful partings,
>> When they left you here below.
>> One by one their seats were emptied,
>> One by one they went away;
>> Here the circle has been broken—
>> Will it be complete one day?"

Grandma G. sang without a tear, but she kept glancing to her right at the empty spot where Grandpa G. had always sat.

As the song continued, a little seven-year-old girl slipped out of the pew where she was sitting with her parents and went up and sat with Grandma G. She offered the old lady a stick of gum, and Grandma G. took it with a smile. Next, a lanky teen with blond curls ambled his way to Grandma G's pew. Reaching around the little girl, he put his arm across Grandma G's shoulder. She smiled at him. Soon the short pew in the country church was so full Grandma G. barely had room to sit when the hymn was finished.

The sermon felt unusually long to the congregation who'd been smelling chicken, baked beans, smoked brisket, and roast beef wafting in from the fellowship area. Finally, the pastor said his last "Amen," and the lanky teen sitting with Grandma G. offered to help her to her car.

"Help me to my car?" she asked. "I haven't been able to attend a potluck at this church since I was seventeen. Grandpa G. hated them, you know. I wouldn't miss this one for the world. You can go to my car and bring in my picnic basket. I baked three pies for today: pumpkin, black raspberry, and cherry."

Grandma G. never missed another potluck until she went to join the heavenly circle when she was one-hundred-and three. And until then, every Sunday, her pew—left side, third from the front—was so full she barely had room to sit.

3
HER NAME WAS ROSE

I found the yellowed paper in an old coupon holder, and, though the words were forty years old, the memory stung like yesterday.

Only two words were legible, and one of those was misspelled: "PLSEASE" and "ROSE." The rest was scribbled in pretend, kindergarten cursive.

Rose called us Mommy and Daddy; though, we were only her babysitters. We didn't know much about her background, only that she was in the foster system and had come from an abusive situation. Her two-year-old sister, Kim, left us each morning to go for therapy.

We had Rose every weekday until she left for afternoon kindergarten. She followed me everywhere, curly, dark brown hair framing her adorable face, blue eyes sparkling with a love of life. She had to "help" do whatever I did.

One day, John heard Rose helping me fold laundry. She held up a pair of his tighty-whities, stretched it out to its full length, and giggled.

"Mommy! Daddy got *big* bottom."

John pulled me aside.

"Please, don't let her fold my underwear."

I laughed.

That little chatterbox was my shadow. I read her all kinds of books, and she loved Bible stories. I didn't ask her about her past; I'd been told not to, and she never volunteered any information.

We had to feed Rose lunch before Kim came home so Rose would be ready for the kindergarten bus. Lunch time was a ritual that never varied.

As soon as we finished thanking God for the food, Rose asked, "What's for zert?"

If we had dessert, we told her what it was. If we didn't have any, she never fussed or complained.

Next, she always took one bite of food, put down her fork and asked, "Is there enough food for Kim?"

I assured her there was.

She nodded, took another bite of food, and asked again, "Is there enough food for Kim?"

I told her there was more than enough food for Kim.

I knew what was coming because it happened every day.

One more bite of food, and then she looked at me and asked in a small, worried voice, "Can I see it?"

Her little hand in mine, I took her to the kitchen and showed her Kim's food. Only then could she enjoy her lunch.

No one had to tell me that, for two of her five years, Rose had been looking out for her two-year-old sister.

We already had three children in a house too small: two boys and a girl. They all slept in the same room divided by a half wall their dad had built, but I fell in love with Rose and Kim and often told John I wished I could keep them. I was happy for them, though; the people we babysat for planned to adopt them, and they were good people.

When Rose left and Kim came home, it was quieter. Kim was non-verbal and not potty trained, but after a while both of those things changed. She liked to be held and rocked and took a long nap every afternoon.

Once, when we lived at that little house, a spring storm came out of nowhere. It snapped a dozen or so trees off at rooftop level and ended before we had a chance to realize it had begun.

It was like that with Rose and Kim. We found out they were not going to be adopted but were going back into the foster system. I immediately called and asked if we could adopt them. The social worker I spoke to was kind but firm. We hadn't even been approved as foster parents, and there were already qualified people on a list, some who wanted Rose, some who wanted Kim. My heart sank. The girls were not going to be staying together. What would they do without each other?

Kim would never remember us, but Rose would. We bought her a Bible storybook—like the one our kids had, the one she loved me to read to her; we signed it with our love.

Rose asked me to keep her. I told her I'd tried, but it couldn't happen. She looked at me with unbelieving eyes, clouds covering the usually sparkling blue.

On their last day with us, Rose gave me a note. Only two words were legible, and one of those was misspelled: "PLSEASE" and "ROSE." The rest was scribbled in pretend, kindergarten cursive.

"I will read it to you," Rose said. "It says, 'Mommy, if you love me, you will keep me.'"

Those words burned into my heart.

Rose, wherever you are, I hope you understand now. I did keep you and Kim in my heart, and I will forever. I still have your note. It's torn now at the folds because it's so old, but I remember your voice reading it to me as though it were yesterday.

Some years later, God sent us a surprise, a fourth baby. We named her Kimberlee, and for many years we called her Kim.

Today I prayed for another Kim, and for her older sister, my little chatterbox, Rose. God bless and keep you both, wherever you are.

4
HOME FOR CHRISTMAS

My husband, John, and his mom were very close. From his first Christmas when he was not even two months old until he was sixty-five, the last Christmas his mom was alive, he never missed spending Christmas with her. The celebration didn't always happen on Christmas Day; sometimes it took place during the week between Christmas and New Year's, but never later. Locations changed from year to year, but they were usually in New York.

John is a pastor, so we never missed our church Christmas programs. But we left soon after with echoes of "Away in the Manger" and visions of crooked tinsel halos still vivid in our minds. The trips east or south were crazy; we were exhausted, and traveling down under Lake Erie with its winter squalls was an adventure.

When John and I were in Bible college in Iowa, we once drove all night through a blizzard to get to New York for Christmas.

The year our firstborn was five months old, we drove

nonstop from Indiana to Georgia to celebrate family Christmas in the south where John's sister lived.

When our firstborn was two-and-a half, another baby was due at Christmas, so John's family travelled to Michigan and stayed with us. John Jr. was born December 27.

Whether Christmas was at our home or we traveled somewhere else, getting everything done was a challenge.

Once I hooked a rug as a gift, barely looking up from our Michigan driveway until we pulled into Mom and Dad Poole's driveway in New York.

Glory to God in the highest, peace on earth and good will to men, and how in the world am I going to get all this done on time?

"Tell John you aren't going to travel any more at Christmas," my sister, Eve, said. "It's too busy of a time, and the weather is awful. We only go out to New York to see family in the summer."

"I can't," I told her. "You don't know what this means to John."

Our three oldest children loved traveling over the river and through the woods to Grandma and Grandpa's house. They had cousins their age and many adventures to remember and new ones to plan. Our youngest daughter came along when the first three were teens or almost teens, and she had no cousins her age. When the group of cousins left to have their Christmas vacation adventures, she was stuck with the old folks. She didn't enjoy the holiday quite as much as they did; though, she dearly loved her grandparents.

Depending on when we traveled for Christmas, we sometimes couldn't have our own family Christmas or open stockings until we got home. That concerned our youngest one. How would Santa know where to find her? I still have two of her notes to Santa from that time:

"Dear Santa,
Please come to my Grandma and Grandpas house on Christmas Eve.
Merry Christmas:
Love
Kimberlee.
P.S. Please wake me up. I want to ask you something."

"Dear Santa,
Please put my gifts on the end of my bed.
I love you.
Love
Kimberlee Joy Poole
P.S. Please check on my kitten. Tell her I miss her and Merry Christmas. Tell her I'll have a Blue Christmas without her."

Things changed when Mom and Dad got older. They moved from New York to Georgia, so John and I drove from Michigan to Georgia every Christmas. Our children were grown then, but some of them went with us every year, including Kimberlee Joy Poole who, by then, would have had a "Blue Christmas" without her grandparents.

After Dad celebrated his last Christmas on earth, Mom spent winters with John's sister in Georgia and summers with us in Michigan. Our Christmas travels ended because the Georgia family brought Mom to Michigan for Christmas. They always hoped to see snow.

Things changed again when Mom got too feeble to travel anymore. A deep infection that needed constant care sent her to a nursing home not far from us where she spent her last three Christmases. We celebrated in her room there with her.

Now John has had to celebrate eight Christmases without his mom, but they will spend an eternity of them together in heaven praising the Baby in the manger who grew up to be the Man on the cross.

Looking back, I don't regret the effort it took to be sure a son was with his mom every Christmas. We have grown children now who move the proverbial heaven and earth to be with us to celebrate family Christmas, and it means more to me every year.

We gather together, crowded into our living room. John and I are the old grandma and grandpa now. A grandson opens the Bible and begins reading from Luke 2, "And it came to pass in those days...."

And my memories race back to Christmas when I was a little girl, and my dad read those same words. I remember all the happy Christmas days when our children were young, and John read those verses. I look at our grandson, reading from God's Word now, and I'm grateful. Grateful for family, grateful for Christmas, grateful for a God who so loved the world He became man so He could die for our sin and make a way for us to go Home. Home for Christmas, Home for eternity.

5
THE SCHOOL BUS RIDE

It seemed a long time ago Debbie had gotten on the school bus as a five-year-old. She'd barely been able to climb the metal steps with her short, chubby legs. She'd dropped her lunch pail, a hand-me-down one from her brother. It had been red metal with a black leather carrying strap. Hopalong Cassidy had smiled from the yellow picture in the center.

"Here you go," the bus driver had said as he handed the lunch pail back to her. "Go sit down now."

Sit down? Where?

She'd stood trembling in the middle of the aisle. All the seats were full. What should she do? Two little girls had scooted close together.

"You can sit with us," one had called.

And so, she had.

"I'm Audrey," one girl had told her.

The other one had giggled. "No, she's not. I'm Audrey. She's Kathy."

"What's in your lunchbox?" Kathy had asked.

"Peanut butter and banana sandwich."

"Really? Me too!"

"I have the same thing!" Audrey had said.

The three little girls had smiled at each other as though they'd just discovered life in outer space.

And what's friendship all about if it's not about the "me too's" and shared discoveries along the way?

∽

It took a long time to get to school as the bus crawled along the winding dirt roads.

"I'm hungry," Debbie said. "I was too scared to eat breakfast."

"I ate my breakfast," Audrey said. "But I was so nervous I threw up. Right on my brother's plate!"

They laughed so hard, other children turned to look at them.

"I didn't eat my breakfast either," Kathy said. "Let's eat our lunches now!"

"But what will we eat at lunchtime?"

Kathy shrugged. "The teacher will probably give us something. Mama promised me the teacher would be kind."

And so, the three opened metal lunchboxes and ate their lunches.

Kindergarten lunch time came.

"Bow your heads, children," Miss Jennings said.

Back in the 1950s, teachers often prayed with children before lunch.

The class recited in unison: "God is great. God is good. And we thank Him for our food. Amen."

It didn't take Miss Jennings long to notice Debbie, Audrey, and Kathy had no lunches.

She didn't scold them when she found out why, just told them, "Next time, wait and eat lunch at school."

Then she took three bright red apples off her desk and gave one to each girl, and she gave every child a tiny carton of milk and a straw.

The girls sat together on the bus on the way home.

"Do you like apples?" Debbie asked the other two.

"Hate them!"

"Me too!"

The girls giggled.

"Do you like milk?" Kathy asked.

"No!" Audrey said.

Debbie shook her head. "And there was a dead fly in mine!"

"Barf!" the other two exclaimed.

"I don't know why the lunch prayer doesn't rhyme," Debbie said. "Mom taught me how to rhyme. 'Food' doesn't rhyme with 'good.'"

"Let's make it rhyme tomorrow," Kathy said. "Let's say, 'God is great. God is good. And we thank Him for our *fude*.'"

They did that every day; only they said it softly, so no one heard them. Then they grinned at each other when prayer was finished.

Once Kathy asked, "Do you think God is mad at us for messing up His prayer?"

Debbie shook her head. "I think He laughs."

"You think God laughs?"

"Yep!"

"Audrey, do you think God laughs?"

"I don't know. I have to think about it."

"I don't think He laughs," Kathy said. "But I'll think about it too, and I'll ask my mom."

And so, the three friends learned something else. Friendship is more than "me too." It's sometimes making each other think.

~

Days, months, and years passed. Debbie, Audrey, and Kathy became friends with everyone on the yellow bus; though, the three of them remained the closest.

They finished high school. One of them finished college. Kathy had twelve children. But still, every day, they rode the yellow bus, as did all their other friends. No one seemed to think it was strange to keep riding the boss.

Years passed; the bus began to make stops at a perpetually foggy intersection. Someone got off, and that someone never got on the bus again. Conversation quieted on the bus for a time then, and there were tears.

Finally, there were only three passengers left on the bus, three very old ladies, Debbie, Audrey, and Kathy. When the bus stopped at the foggy intersection, Audrey and Kathy grabbed hands and smiled. They hugged Debbie and left the bus together.

For many days, Debbie sat alone and cried. There was no one left to talk to.

~

It seemed a long time ago Debbie had gotten on the school bus as a five-year-old. She'd barely been able to climb the metal steps with her short, chubby legs. She'd dropped her lunch pail, a hand-me-down one from her brother. It had been red metal with a black leather carrying strap. Hopalong Cassidy had smiled from the yellow picture in the center.

∼

DEBBIE MOVED up and took a seat right behind the driver. "Do you have any idea how long ago I got on your bus?"

"As a matter of fact, I do. You got on eighty-five years ago today."

"I'd like to get off now, if you wouldn't mind stopping at the foggy intersection."

He shook his head. "Sorry. I don't have permission to make that stop yet."

It was quiet for many days after that. One thing changed, though. Debbie didn't sit in the back anymore; she sat as close to the driver as she could get.

One day, Debbie opened the lunch she'd brought with her and bit into her peanut butter and banana sandwich.

"Do you think God laughs?" she asked the driver.

The driver chuckled. "I know He does, and I know something else. Today is the day you've been waiting for."

"You mean...."

He nodded. With a creaking sound the old bus stopped, and the doors opened. The driver stood and helped Debbie down the stairs. She stood there a minute. The fog parted, and she saw Audrey and Kathy waiting for her. From somewhere behind them, she heard laughter, the kind of beautiful laughter that says welcome Home.

Debbie turned to thank the driver. He raised a hand to wave goodbye, and she saw a scar.

Is that a nail print? So, He's been my driver all along?

He called to her, "Don't worry. Your teacher will be very kind, and there won't be any dead flies in your milk."

NOTES

Here We Go Again!

1. 1 Corinthians 12:13

Lion and Lamb

1. Isaiah 11:6

Let Freedom Ring

1. John 8:36

Summer Sun Was on His Wings, Winter in His Cry

1. Isaiah 53:3
2. Hebrews 1:9
3. Colossians 1:16-17

ABOUT THE AUTHOR

"Mom," Donna's tired son once said to her as he walked with her, "you don't have to hike every trail in this park."

"Yes, I do."

"But why?"

"Because."

Just because. If a trail was there, Donna had to hike it. Hiking was one of her passions, along with reading, sitting around a campfire with family and friends, and writing.

Donna can no longer hike; the short distance from the car to the house exhausts her. She's fighting cancer, so now all her backroad ramblings are virtual.

Donna's writing career began in 1973 when she sold her first short story. Since then, she has sold more than 3,000 articles and short stories and has published several books available on Amazon. She's a member of American Christian Fiction Writers.

Donna and her husband John live in Michigan and are parents of four grown, married children, and grandparents to fourteen amazing grandchildren. They've been married for fifty-three years. For forty-eight of those years, John has been pastor of a small country church.

Donna appreciates her readers and thanks each one of them!

If you enjoy this or any of Donna's books, please consider leaving a review on Amazon.

You can find Donna's blog at backroadramblings.com. Find out more about Donna on Facebook at "Donna Poole, author."

Printed in Great Britain
by Amazon